CROSSED AND FOUND

MYSTERY HISTORY
– BOOK ONE –

By Sonny Barber

Washington Crossing State Park in Hopewell Township, New Jersey is an amazing resource on the history of the American Revolution and especially the critical battles and events that took place in the area. This story is fiction based partly on historical figures and places from that locale and on that era.

In the present day story setting, names, characters, businesses, places, events and incidents are either the products of the author's imagination or used in a fictitious manner. Any resemblance to actual persons, living or dead, or actual events is purely coincidental.

Cover design by AuthorSupport.com

Copyright © 2014 Sonny Barber
All Rights Reserved.

ISBN-13: 9781495304057
ISBN-10: 1495304051
Library of Congress Control Number: 2014901580
CreateSpace Independent Publishing Platform
North Charleston, South Carolina

To my wife, my best friend, Barbara.

CHAPTER ONE

December 22, 1776, near the Delaware River in New Jersey

"I'm coming!" the young girl yelled. The ferry master's fourteen-year-old daughter scurried across the room, lifted the bolt, and opened the heavy door. Her father and his passenger traipsed through with snow swirling around their legs. Hiding behind the door to avoid the wintry blast, the girl quickly closed it after them. "How was the crossing?"

The lanky ferry master removed his coat and hat. "Treacherous and miserable. I thought the ice would tear a hole in the boat."

A black kettle simmered above the glowing coals of the fireplace and filled the room with the aroma of meat and potato stew.

Helping her father at the inn since her mother had died a year earlier, Elizabeth approached the passenger. He was a gray-haired man who held tight to a small leather bag.

The young girl asked, "Would you like something to eat, sir?"

"Yes, thank you," he said. The man stood at the fireplace and pointed to the bubbling cauldron. "I'll have some of this stew and some tea."

The girl stared at the man. Heat from the fire softened the gray creases in his face. The rosiness slowly returned to his cheeks. The man wiped his face with a kerchief and handed the young teen his hat and cape.

She hung the items on hooks and walked over to her father. Shooting a glance back at the man, Elizabeth asked, "Who is he?"

1

Her father drew her close and whispered, "I don't know, and I'm not going to ask. The soldier who arranged the passage said it would be dangerous for me to know the man's name."

Poking the fire and sweeping the hearth, Elizabeth caught glimpses of the mysterious passenger, who slowly ate and sipped his tea.

An hour passed. She watched from the top of the stairs. The passenger drummed his fingers on the table, alternating his gaze between his pocket watch and the door.

The teen came downstairs and approached the man. "Can I get you some more stew or tea?"

"No, thanks. I must return across the river soon."

"Sir, my father says he may close the ferry because of the ice. And he does not like crossing in the darkness either."

The man took a sip of tea, placed his cup on the table, and stood. "Then we must leave now."

Hearing the man, the ferry master scurried in from the other room. He put on his coat and hat, removed the bolt from the door, and waited for his passenger.

Elizabeth gave the man his hat and cape.

He reached into his leather bag and pulled out a piece of paper, folded and sealed with a lump of crimson wax. "A rider will come for this letter. You must give it to him. If he does not arrive by morning, please destroy it. Your lives may be in grave danger if you should know the contents."

The girl's eyes widened. Her heart raced. She took the paper in both hands and carefully placed it on the mantle.

● ● ●

Closing the door, the ferry master raked the snow from his coat and grumbled. "Awful weather."

"You must read this," his daughter said. The letter fluttered between her fingers.

Her father's eyes bugged. "Why did you open it?"

"I didn't. The heat must have loosened the seal."

2

Gripping a glowing candle, the ferry master took the letter, and read it. "Why would…is the war going so badly that—"

Elizabeth touched his arm. "Listen! A rider!"

The muffled clop of a horse's hooves in the snow grew louder.

The ferry master folded the letter. The color drained from his face. His hands trembled, and his voice was weak. "Where's the seal? Without it, he'll think we read the letter."

"I don't have the seal. It fell off when I took the letter off the mantle. I couldn't find it."

His mouth hung open as he gazed at the letter.

"Father, are you all right?"

No response.

She tugged at his arm. "Father! Father!"

He continued to gaze at the document.

"We must burn the letter!" she cried.

The ferry master stood silent and still as stone. He stared, glassy-eyed at the paper.

Elizabeth gently eased the letter from his hands, knelt at the fireplace, and stared at the glowing coals. What if the man who came for the letter sees it burning?

Removing several loose bricks from the corner of the fireplace, she reached in the place where her father sometimes hid coins from the British. She pulled out a metal tube, shoved the tightly rolled letter into it, and rammed the heavy container back into the hole. A deep clunking sound echoed. Fingers outstretched, the young girl thrust her hand into the narrow tunnel—deeper than ever before. She touched the edge of an open space, but found no tube. She had pushed it too far. The young girl tried to pull her arm out of the tunnel, but it was stuck.

"Innkeeper!" The rider stomped his boots and banged on the door.

The ferry master shook his head and wiped his eyes as if awakening from a trance. He waved at his daughter and gave a loud whisper. "Hurry."

Elizabeth pulled back again. Her hand slid back by a few inches, but was caught again. With a final skin-tearing yank, she freed herself and replaced the bricks.

"Innkeeper!"

The ferry master lifted the bolt and slowly opened the door. Its rusty hinges squeaked and echoed inside the room.

Elizabeth cringed, her face taut.

"Did you not hear me?" The soldier stepped through the doorway and brushed past the ferry master. Standing well over six feet tall, he whirled his cape off his shoulders and revealed his uniform. Its shiny buttons and gold lacework stood out from the drab gray and brown colors of the inn.

Elizabeth whispered to her father, "He sounds strange. He's not an English soldier, is he?"

"He's a Hessian—a mercenary hired to fight us."

Pacing across the room, the soldier whipped his head around. "Did you say something?"

"No...Yes...I was telling my daughter to watch the stew; it's boiling."

The soldier glanced up the stairs and walked over to the fireplace. After facing the burning coals and warming his hands, the soldier pivoted. He fixed his gaze first on the ferry master. The Hessian's blue eyes widened. He jerked his head to the right and looked at Elizabeth.

In one quick motion, she lowered her head to avoid the soldier's stare.

The wax seal! With a quick glance, she saw him again turn toward the fireplace. She slowly bent her knees, reached down, and picked up the lump of wax. As she rose, she saw the bowl, spoon, and cup on the table where the stranger had eaten. Would the soldier notice? Her hands shook. She carefully placed the items in the trough of her apron and inched away from the table.

"I was to meet someone. Did you say no one has been here this evening?" Facing away from the Hessian, Elizabeth stopped in mid-stride, her legs like rubber. The dishes rattled. She flashed a look at her father.

The ferry master shook his head, the movements barely notice-able.

His daughter swallowed hard, her mouth as dry as a desert. "No, sir, there's been no one here this evening."

"Perhaps I should wait. There may have been difficulty getting to the inn."

Her heart pounding, Elizabeth took a deep breath and exhaled slowly. "Where was he coming from?"

The soldier touched his finger to his top lip and stared expressionless at the girl. "From across the river."

"He won't be coming tonight," the ferry master said. "I've closed the ferry. There's too much ice on the Delaware, and the wind's picking up."

Lowering his head, the soldier squinted at the ferry master and turned toward the young girl.

She clasped her hands to stop them from shaking.

The soldier pointed at the simmering cauldron. "May I purchase some of that stew?"

Twenty minutes passed. The soldier finished his meal and left the inn.

Elizabeth replaced the bolt and stood with her back against the door, breathing rapidly and listening. The muted and rhythmic clip-clop of the horse faded. "He's gone."

The ferry master dashed to the fireplace and knelt on the hearth.

Elizabeth shook her head. "It's no use."

The ferry master stopped tugging at the bricks. "What do you mean?"

"The tube fell back into a hole when I put it in. I couldn't reach it. It's gone."

"Gone? Are you sure?"

"Yes." The girl slid her hands into her apron pockets. She felt the wax seal, pulled it out, and showed it to her father.

He pointed at the fire.

She tossed the seal into the flames and ran to him, wrapping her arms around his thin frame.

Embracing his daughter, the ferry master kissed her on the top of her head and said softly, "We must tell no one about the letter—ever."

CHAPTER TWO

Summer, The Park at Washington Crossing

Kay Telfair rubbed her hands along the glass-cased displays. "Bor-ring," the thirteen-year-old said, stopping at one of the Revolutionary War exhibits.

A tall woman with large glasses and standing with a young, bushy brown-haired boy glared at Kay. "American history is not boring. It's exciting, as well as important."

Kay blushed.

The woman pointed out artifacts and read aloud the information on the plaques beneath an item. The young boy rolled his eyes at Kay and offered a half wave.

Kay shrugged and shuffled slowly along the row of exhibits.

"Why are *you* here?" a voice from behind her asked.

Kay jumped back, nearly colliding with the young boy who had been standing with the tall woman. "You scared me."

The boy winced. "Didn't mean to. My name's Jason. What's yours?"

"Kay."

"Why did you come to the park?"

"My mom made me. We've been unpacking boxes for a week. She said we needed to get out of the house."

Jason stared through one of the glass-topped counters. "These buttons are neat. Some are made of wood." He turned toward Kay. "What are you unpacking?"

Kay sighed. "Things."

"What things?"

Kay gave the boy her famous eye roll and huff. "We're unpacking everything we own. My mom, dad, and me—we moved here from Florida a few weeks ago. From Tallahassee."

Kay inched slowly along the display cases.

The boy followed. "Why did you move to New Jersey?"

Kay's mouth drooped. "My dad's job."

"How do you like living in Jersey so far?"

"Sucks." Kay winced and whipped her head around. Her mom didn't like her using that word. She looked at Jason. "Do you live in New Jersey?"

The boy glanced around the room and waved at his mom. "I live in Pennsylvania—in Doylestown."

Kay eyed her mom across the room. "Why did you come to the park?"

"My mom wants to bring her class here on a field trip, and she wanted to check it out."

"Is your mom your teacher?"

"Next year. She teaches seventh grade."

Kay shook her head. "I can't imagine what it would be like if my mom were my teacher."

"My sister was in my mom's class a few years ago. I guess it won't be too bad."

"Have you lived in Doylesville—"

The boy raised his finger. "Town."

"How long have you lived in Doyles*town*?"

"All my life."

"Lucky you. I left all my friends in Tallahassee after living there for six years. This is our third move since I was born."

"You'll make new friends, I'm sure."

Kay spun around and faced Jason. "I don't need to make new friends."

The boy stepped back, his thick, brown eyebrows arching over his glasses.

Kay half smiled and softened her tone. "What I meant was I was planning on going to high school in Florida. Now everything's changed. I loved living there, and I hate cold weather."

Jason shrugged. "It's not cold now."

Kay nodded and smiled. "How cold does it—"

"I have to go." Jason looked over at his mom, who motioned to him.

"Nice talking to you." He walked away and joined his mom at the door of the visitor center.

Kay muttered. "And nice talking to you, too, Doylesville—city—town—whatever."

A young woman pointed to the displays and tugged on her male companion's arm. "The ranger said there was a break-in at the visitor center. Some of these things are valuable, but how would you know what to take?"

The companion pointed. "Look at the gold buttons and antique guns in perfect condition. Why didn't they take these things?"

Kay inched closer to the couple and stared at the display. A book and framed papers with plaques describing the items remained in the case. Above some plaques were empty holders and faint outlines of the missing items on the faded gray-cloth background.

The young woman waved her hand in the direction of the semicircular reception desk. "The man said the alarm didn't go off for some reason. The broken glass cut one of the burglars. That's why the carpet has a stain on it."

"Yuck." Kay maneuvered around the yellow warning sign on the floor and on to another display. "Who cares about all this stuff anyway?" Threading her long, straight hair behind her ears, she leaned on the plywood that replaced the broken glass to get a better view. The edges rubbed together and made a loud, popping sound that echoed across the room.

In ten short steps, Kay's mom stood beside her daughter. "Please be careful."

"I hate this place, Mom. I hate New Jersey. I hate—" Kay didn't want to say those last words. They weren't true. Her mother was her only close friend now.

Her mom said, "I'm going to the gift shop. Do you want to come?"

Kay shook her head. "No, thanks." She wandered over to the information desk and picked up a brochure. Loud voices on the other side of a nearby closed door caught her attention.

"Your security alarm didn't go off. Whoever was supposed to turn it on forgot."

"I manage this place the best I can with the money they give me. I'm lucky I have somebody like Eddie at the reception desk. He's retired and puts in more hours than we pay him for."

Kay took small side steps and inched closer to the door. Somebody was mad.

"All I know is that you're the superintendent here, and you're responsible."

"After seventeen years of dedication to the park service and being on call twenty-four hours a day, *I'm* going to be the fall guy?"

"I'm not saying what's going to happen. You were in charge when the thefts took place. The FBI probably will get involved since most of the stolen artifacts came from the Smithsonian. And watch out for Millie Richards. She's written two letters to me about the displays not being repaired, and she blamed the staff here both times. Don't forget, she *is* the wife of a US senator. I'm sure she's given him an earful."

The angry voices stopped. The handle jiggled. Kay expected the door to be pulled back into whatever room existed behind it. But the door came careening into the space where she stood.

"Owwwwww!" The door struck the left side of Kay's head above her eye. She staggered, arms outstretched, and sat hard on the floor.

One of the men peeked around the door. "What did I do?" He dropped his folder, papers flying across the floor, and shouted to the ranger behind the desk. "Eddie, get me the first-aid kit and call 9-1-1!"

Kay moaned and touched her head. The man knelt beside her as another man peered over his shoulder and half chuckled. "Nice work. I don't think I've ever known a park superintendent who knocked over one of his visitors."

"Lie back." The park superintendent pressed a handkerchief against the small cut on Kay's brow. He put his arm at her back and eased her to the floor.

"Kay!" her mom yelled, running across the room. Kneeling beside her daughter, she pulled a tissue pack from her purse and dabbed at the blood. She looked up at the man holding her daughter's head.

"I'm Rich Gardino, the superintendent of the park. I'm really sorry."

"What happened?" Kay's mom asked.

"I pushed the door open and it hit her," Rich said. "I didn't know she was standing so close." Rich turned when the ranger walked up to the group with the first aid kit. He barked orders to the gray-haired man. "Hold her head, Eddie, while I put on this bandage. Don't let her move until the paramedics get here." He yanked off the backing of the large adhesive bandage and pressed it against Kay's head. "How're you doing, young lady?"

"My head hurts."

Her hands trembling, Kay's mom eased beside the ranger and cupped her hands beneath Kay's head. "You'll be fine. Lie still."

Ten minutes passed. A female paramedic carrying a large red case touched the superintendent's shoulder. "Make way. Excuse me. I need to get through." A male paramedic followed.

The female leaned over Kay.

Kay's mom glanced up at the medic. "Her name's Kay."

"Kay, I'm Loretta." The medic lifted the bandage, examined the cut, and ran her fingers around to the back of Kay's neck.

Rich leaned over the medic. "It's my fault. I was so anxious to—"

"We may have a concussion and maybe a neck injury," Loretta said, her voice echoing across the room. She called out to the other medic. "Bring the stretcher."

The medics gently lifted Kay onto the stretcher and covered her with a blanket.

"Mom?"

"Yes, dear, I'm here."

"What's happening?"

Loretta touched Kay's arm. "We're taking you to the hospital. Your mom can ride in the back of the ambulance with us."

Out in the parking lot, Loretta climbed into the white-and-orange vehicle. She checked Kay's pulse and pumped on the blood pressure cuff. "Do you live nearby?"

Kay squeezed her mom's hand. The ambulance rocked as it rolled out of the parking lot and sped up. "Not too far. We moved here last week from Florida."

Loretta nodded at Kay's mom and smiled at the teen. "Welcome to New Jersey, Kay. Let's hope the rest of your time here is not quite so exciting—or dangerous."

CHAPTER THREE

"This is Mr. Gardino's daughter," Kay's mom said. "Mr. Gardino came to visit you in the hospital. Remember?"

Kay folded her arms. "I think so. You're Anna, right?""

Anna spoke through lips partially closed to hide her braces. "That's me. My dad told me what happened. He still feels awful. Does it hurt?"

"Not anymore."

"I thought you might want to go for a bike ride. We can ride around and see the area. I'll show you where I live. It's not too far."

"I don't know. I'm a little tired."

Kay's mother glared at her.

Anna smiled at Kay's mom and shifted her gaze to Kay. "My dad told me you came here from Florida. I've been to Florida a few times. I wish *I* lived there. They say it's nice, especially in the winter."

"I wish I was there now."

Anna blushed and cleared her throat.

"Anna came over here to meet you." Kay's mom's voice rose. "You said you were tired of being in the house."

Kay sighed and walked toward the stairs. "OK, I'll go."

"Kay's not herself. The move and—"

"Mom, I'm fine," Kay called out. "I'll be right down."

Five minutes later, Kay stood at the bottom of the stairs. "I'm ready."

"Nice meeting you, Anna," Kay's mom said.

"Thanks. It was nice meeting—"

"Can we go, please?" Kay asked, slipping on her bike helmet.

Bathed in a warm summer breeze, the girls pedaled down the tree-lined streets through Kay's new neighborhood.

"Before I show you where I live, let's go down to the river. It's cooler there."

Kay tilted her head up at the blue sky filled with white, cotton-candy clouds. Her mind wandered to all the bike rides she and her dad made in their neighborhood in Tallahassee.

The girls biked past the entrance to the park and down to River Road near the Washington Crossing Bridge. Anna stopped her bike in front of the convenience store at the intersection. "I need something to drink. Can I get you a soda or water?"

"Thanks. Just water."

The girls sipped their drinks while sitting under a large oak tree near the store. Neither spoke for a few minutes.

Anna broke the ice. "I'm guessing you don't have any brothers or sisters. Your mom didn't—"

"You got it. Only me, here, alone in New Jersey."

"I have a brother, Buddy. He's a pain."

"At least you *have* a brother."

Anna stood, dusting off the seat of her shorts. "Maybe this bike ride wasn't such a good idea."

"Sorry. It's just that I feel like I'm alone up here. Maybe having a brother or sister would make it better." Kay downed the last few sips of her water and walked over to the recycling bin. She stood three inches taller than Anna. The two couldn't be mistaken for sisters, and Kay wasn't sure they would ever be friends.

After another awkward few minutes of silence, Kay said, "In Tallahassee, in the summer when I rode my bike, I sweated a lot. We had a thunderstorm every afternoon. But I loved it there." Kay paused, surveying her surroundings. "I left all my friends and my school." She flicked away a few small tears and regained her composure.

Anna searched her pockets and took out a packet of tissues. "Here, you can have these."

"Thanks." Kay wiped the tears and sniffed, turning away.

"I wish I could say I understand, but I don't...I mean, I can't." Anna paused and sipped her soda. "I've lived in Jersey all my life. My dad has worked at only two parks. We've never had to move since I was born. He's been at Washington Crossing for about five years. I wish we had lived in a few other places."

Kay shook her head, avoiding Anna's gaze. "Moving is not that great. You have to make new friends and get used to a new school." Pulling out her phone, Kay swiped at the screen, never moving her focus from the device while she spoke. "I don't even get any texts or e-mails from my friends in Florida." She glanced at Anna for a few seconds, lowered her head, and tapped the screen. "Some of my friends made fun of me when I told them I was moving to New Jersey."

"We get laughed at a lot here in Jersey. People think we're all like those reality-TV-show people. Both my parents are from Jersey."

Kay swiped at the phone while another minute passed with no conversation. After a dozen quick taps on the screen, she said, "I expected to get some e-mails from at least one or two of my friends on my swim team. I got an e-mail the first week we got here. Nothing since."

Anna fiddled with her bike helmet. "Maybe the cell service isn't working or the e-mail system's having problems."

Kay shoved the phone into her pocket. "You think you have friends, but the way to find out is to move away. A lot of these people—we swam together; we hung out. I don't get it."

"I have people here in Jersey—mostly girls—that I've known for years. One day they're my friend, and the next they don't want anything to do with me. There are a few who are nice to me, but I don't get included in some things."

Kay adjusted the strap on her bike helmet. "Why is that? Why do some people treat others that way?"

Anna's tone softened. "I don't know, but it hurts."

"It sure does." Kay sighed and stared off into the distance.

"Come on," Anna said. "Let's ride." She pointed at the nine-hundred-foot-long Washington Crossing Bridge, a maze of intersecting steel girders weaving a path across the Delaware River. "If nobody's on the walkway, we can ride our bikes. We're not supposed to, but during the week, there aren't many people walking the bridge. Besides, the road's too narrow for us if cars are coming."

Anna traveled about fifty feet, stopped, and looked back at Kay.

Kay had stopped and was straddling her bike.

Anna yelled, "What's wrong?"

"Nothing. I'm fine. Give me a minute."

"We don't have to do this. We can cross the bridge some other time when we're riding. It can be kind of scary."

The narrow passage made it impossible to turn around. Anna got off her bike and half carried and half rolled it back to Kay. "Why don't we put the bikes over here and walk out a ways?"

The girls leaned the bikes on the guardrail and ambled twenty-five yards out onto the narrow wooden path. Anna stopped and leaned on the rail. "It's a great view, isn't it?"

Kay nodded and nearly broke a smile. For the moment, her fears vanished. The dampness enveloped her. She drew her arms up, held them close, and inhaled the sweet smell of wildflowers blooming along the river. "This *is* nice. Very relaxing."

A roaring sound echoed through the bridge. Kay recoiled and whipped her head left and right.

Anna pivoted in the direction of the noise. "It's the tires. They make that sound on the road because it's all metal. You can see right through it down to the river."

Kay peered over the inside rail, staring through the grate at the river seventy feet below. Her heart pounded. She breathed faster and shallower. Kay relished thrill rides and considered herself a daredevil on her bike, sometimes resulting in disaster. She had sported a broken wrist at age seven after jumping a dirt mound. At ten, she fractured her wrist riding her bike in the woods. But the bridge was different from her bike stunts or amusement-park adventures. It intimidated her.

Anna tapped Kay on the arm. "Let's go. We can try the bridge some other time. I promised my mom I'd be home by four o'clock."

Pedaling a few feet, Kay stopped and wiped her sweaty palms on her capris. She swiveled her head, took in a deep breath, and stared at the mass of metal behind her.

CHAPTER FOUR

"How was your ride?" Kay's mom stood in the doorway.

"It was OK." Kay brushed past her.

"Did you and Anna get along?"

"Yep."

"She seems like a nice girl. Maybe she'll be in some of your classes in the fall."

"Yeah, maybe."

Her mom followed her to the foot of the stairs. "She could be your first new friend here in New Jersey."

Kay stopped on the third step and said, "*My* friends are in Tallahassee!" She trudged up the stairs to her room.

Kay sprawled across the bed, caressing a pillow. "At least I used to have friends there."

Her mom pushed open the door and put her hands on her hips. "Kay, your attitude is not healthy, and it's causing your dad and me more stress than we deserve."

"*You're* stressed? You didn't have to change schools. And you and Dad didn't have many friends anyway."

"That's not fair. Your father made this move to help us. He wouldn't have a job if we'd stayed in Tallahassee. Do you think we like moving?"

Kay buried her head deeper in the pillow.

"By the way, dinner will be ready around five-thirty."

"I don't know if I want dinner. I need a nap."

Mom huffed. "You need to eat, Kay."

"Fine. I'll set my alarm."

Her mom shook her head, turned, and walked out of the room.

• • •

Kay's dad walked into the kitchen. "Where's my Jersey girl?"

"In her room, and please don't call her that," her mom said.

"I'm here. And what's this about a Jersey girl?"

"Nothing. Your dad was just being funny." Her mom rolled her eyes and stared at her dad.

Kay sat at the table. "Can we eat, please?"

"Your mom tells me you met the park superintendent's daughter. Her name is Anna. Right? How did that go?"

"She's nice."

"What did you do?"

"We rode our bikes."

"Where'd you go?"

"Around."

"That tells me a lot."

"We rode to the Washington Crossing Bridge."

"Did you and Anna hit it off?"

Kay laid her fork on the plate. "If you mean are we best friends, the answer is: my friends are in Florida. Where *we* should be."

Her mom took a deep breath and shook her head.

Kay said nothing during the rest of dinner. Her parents chatted about her dad's new job.

"May I please be excused?"

Her mom wiped her mouth with her napkin. "Of course. Will you come help me clear the table when we're done?"

Kay reached the stairs. "I'll be back down in a minute."

Kay's dad leaned toward his wife. "What's with her? I thought she was getting over the move."

Kay stopped before reaching the top of the stairs.

"I thought so, too. We had words today."

"That's not good. How did the two girls get along?"

"Anna was very nice to her; Kay was not very friendly."

"Was Kay rude to her?"

"No, not rude. I can't put my finger on it. Maybe Kay knows that Anna could be her good friend—a best friend even. If she accepts Anna, that would mean losing that last connection with her life in Tallahassee."

Kay's dad took a sip of tea. "What do we do?"

"The only thing I know to do is give her more time to adjust to living here."

Tears rolled down Kay's cheeks as she quietly climbed the remaining steps. She whispered, "Time. Is that what they think I need?"

CHAPTER FIVE

Kay shuffled into the kitchen.

"I thought you were going to sleep all day." Kay's mom peered over the top of her glasses and shifted her eyes. She kept her head angled at the tablet computer. "It's almost ten."

"I would've slept longer, but the phone woke me."

"That was Anna's mom. She invited us over for lunch today."

"Are we going?"

"I accepted the invitation. Do you not want to go?"

"I don't feel very sociable."

Her mom shook her head and reached for her coffee. "You've been out of the water for a while—"

"I know what you're going to say. Getting back in the pool will help my attitude. I get it, Mom."

A few weeks before her fifth birthday, Kay had begun swimming lessons. At six, she joined the school team and had swum through elementary and middle school. She loved the freestyle and performed best in the distance events.

A growth spurt at twelve shot her from five-two to five-six. She was among the taller girls in her eighth-grade class. In swim meets, Kay's height and upper-body strength often gave her faster times than the boys. She complemented the swimming with frequent bike rides to increase the strength in her legs. She hated running, but did it grudgingly. Having seen a triathlete competition on TV a few years ago, Kay had decided that someday she would be a triathlete, which required swimming, biking, and running.

Her mom took a deep breath and exhaled slowly. "It wouldn't hurt. We can join the Y in Princeton and—"

"I don't need to swim. I'm fine."

The strict swim-team regimen after school—and sometimes before—cut into homework and personal time. Kay's attitude and grades always improved during the swim season. She surprised her parents once by telling them at dinner that she couldn't chat because she had to get to her homework.

"How about another bike ride? Have you talked to Anna since?"

"Nope."

"Why not? It was nice of her to spend the afternoon with you and show you around town."

"I don't know if Anna wants to go riding with me again, but I'll ask her when we go for lunch today. How's that?"

"I suppose that will do. Do you want a cup?"

In addition to another piercing in each ear at age twelve, her mom had granted Kay the privilege of drinking coffee. Her mom called it "the nectar of the gods."

"Yes, please. I need it."

"Your grandfather always said he needed a strong cup in the morning to get the meanness out."

Kay barely cracked a smile and poured a cup of the black liquid. "What time are we going?"

"We'll leave at quarter after eleven."

"I need to shower and wash my hair."

"That's up to you. The car's pulling out of the drive at quarter after."

Kay picked up her mug and glared. "Thanks for the notice."

• • •

"Anna! Kay and her mom are here."

Buddy ran into the foyer.

"And this is Anna's brother, Buddy."

Buddy stared at Kay. "I'm ten—almost eleven. Anna told me you were afraid to cross the bridge on your bike."

Kay rolled her eyes.

"Buddy, that's no way to greet our guests."

"I don't like crossing the bridge either—except in a car."

Anna's mom shuffled to the foot of the stairs. "Anna!"

"Coming! Hold on!"

Anna rushed into the dining room and sat next to Buddy at the table. Kay and her mom sat on the other side.

Mrs. Gardino asked Kay's mom, "How's the transition to New Jersey going?"

"Moves are never easy, but we're managing." Kay's mom shot a glance at her.

"I'm sure it's quite different from Tallahassee," Anna's mom said.

"Wait till winter." Buddy put his hands together in a pretend grip imitating a shoveling motion and grinned. "I bet we have more snow than Florida."

Kay shook her head and rolled her eyes. Snow. That was one more thing against the move to New Jersey.

"It's not so bad, you'll—"

"That's enough about shoveling snow," his mom said.

The two moms provided most of the conversation during lunch. Mrs. Gardino poured the coffee and winked at Anna. "If you kids are done, why don't you go into the family room?"

Buddy scurried ahead of the girls. "I've got some video games we can play."

Kay moaned.

Anna rose and folded her napkin. "I need to do some things in my room."

"What things?" Her mom smiled at Kay. "We have guests."

Anna stood by her chair and took a deep breath. "I suppose I can do it later."

"That would be better. By the way, did you take Kay through the park on your ride?"

Anna sighed. "No, Mom, I didn't."

"Then why don't you make plans for another bike ride? We'll clear the table and finish our coffee."

"Come on," Buddy said, tugging at Kay's arm. "I want to show you my new video game."

Kay leaned in while Buddy switched on the game console and fiddled with the controls.

Anna tapped Kay on the shoulder. "Let's go to my room. He'll be in his own world in ten seconds."

Kay sat on the edge of Anna's bed. "Do you have a boyfriend?"

"What? No. I did like this guy last year. Anyway, my mom says I'm too young to date. How about you?"

"Who, me? Heck no. No particular boy, but there were a few that I liked on the swim team. I was getting to know one when my dad told us he got a job in New Jersey. There was another boy I liked, but he was too shy. We had a project together in one of my classes. It was painful." Kay chuckled. "Poor thing. He could barely speak to me."

Anna stood. "We don't have to take a ride to the park if you don't want to."

Kay fiddled with her phone. "I can do it or not. Whatever you want."

Buddy stuck his head into the bedroom. "You left me. What are you talking about? A bike ride? I'll go with you. How about tomorrow?"

Through clenched teeth, Anna raised her voice and said, "Maybe Kay doesn't *want* to ride to the park."

Kay smiled devilishly. "I'd love to take a ride to the park. Buddy can come with us."

Buddy spread his arms, his hands in a mock grip on handlebars. "When are we going?"

Kay looked up from her phone. "I'm available anytime."

Anna tightened her jaw. "Eleven-thirty. Meet us here."

CHAPTER SIX

Kay straddled her bike, took off her helmet, and lifted the hair off her neck. Perspiration trickled down the center of her back. Her knee touched the empty water-bottle holder on her bike frame. "I should have brought something to drink."

Anna adjusted her helmet and fanned herself with her hands. "I didn't think it would be this hot."

Buddy panted. "Why do we have to stop here? The ranger knows the superintendent's our dad."

Before Anna could answer, the park ranger stuck his head out of the gatehouse. "Hello, Anna. Who's your friend? Or maybe she's *your* friend, Buddy."

Buddy blushed.

With a glint in his eye, the ranger focused on Kay. "Is he *your* boyfriend?"

Kay grimaced and squinted at the man.

Anna leaned her bike toward the gatehouse window. "This is Kay. I want to show her the park."

"Hi, Kay. Glad to meet you."

Kay offered the ranger a weak but polite, "Hi."

Buddy pushed his bike ahead and jumped on the seat. The girls followed him down the hill.

The ranger called out, "There's some serious construction going on. Watch out for the trucks. Pull off the road when you see them coming. And stay out of the ferry house. Your dad wouldn't want you in there with all the work being done!"

Anna threw a wave without turning her head.

The two girls pedaled slowly, passing in and out of the shadows beneath the oak and maple trees lining the roadway.

Buddy pedaled faster. "Come on, let's go." Attempting to avoid a pothole left from the winter freeze, he squeezed hard on the brake levers. The bike skidded, fell over at the edge of the pavement, and slid onto the grass.

The girls slowed at the curve, laid the bikes over, and ran over to Buddy.

"Ouch! My leg." Buddy gritted his teeth and winced. Small tears appeared in the corners of his brown eyes.

Kay knelt beside him. "Are you hurt?"

"He's all right." Anna pursed her lips and shook her head.

"I am not. My leg's bleeding."

A nasty scrape showed where his knee had hit the pavement. Grass stains were streaked across his khaki shorts.

"It really burns." He drew his knee up to his chest with both hands. "Do something."

Kay's hand hovered over the scrape.

Buddy pulled away. "Don't touch it."

"Don't worry, I won't. But some water may help. Any in that house?"

Buddy frowned. "We're not supposed to go in there."

"All we need is a little water," Kay said. "We won't be long."

Anna stood, hands on her hips. "Didn't you hear what the ranger said?"

Kay shook her head. "What's the big deal? If nobody's in the house, we can be in and out before anyone knows we were there."

Buddy's eyelids drooped. He dragged his forearm across his face to wipe away the sweat. "Can you carry me?"

Anna glared at her brother. "No, we can't. Get back on your bike, and let's go home. You can get a bandage and some stuff for the pain."

Kay picked up Buddy's bike. "If there's some water in there, it'll only take a minute to wash off his knee. I think I saw a worker leave. He jumped in a truck with some guy. Maybe they went to lunch." She glanced at her phone. "It's almost noon."

"You'll get me in trouble if we go in there," Anna said.

"I only want to help your brother."

Anna gazed to her right and left. "What if my dad finds out?"

Kay shrugged. "He won't know. If there's no one inside, we can go in. We'll be fast."

"I'm already on my dad's bad list. If this gets me grounded—"

"It hurts." Buddy grimaced and hobbled to the house with a steadying hand from the girls.

Kay stuck her head in the door and listened. No sounds. She motioned to Anna and Buddy.

Anna spotted a sink and faucet. She cupped her hands to catch the liquid and poured it over Buddy's knee.

He cried, "That's cold!"

With Anna caring for Buddy's scrape, Kay strolled through the house, peeking under the drop cloths at the antique tables and chairs and opening bins and cupboards. She climbed the stairs and sat at the top. Making a megaphone of her hands over her mouth, Kay faked a deep, gravelly voice. "What are you two doing in here?"

Buddy gasped and jerked his leg. Anna spun around and dumped a handful of water on his shoes.

"Up here," Kay yelled.

"You scared the heck out of me." Anna shook her head. "We need to leave now. I don't want to get caught in here. My dad will kill me. He's been really tense lately…you know, with the burglary at the visitor center."

"Come on up. It's a great view."

"No. You come down."

Kay motioned her friends up the stairs.

Buddy hobbled to the staircase and began climbing.

Anna followed, shaking her head. "Your exasperating, Kay. We shouldn't be up here—or even in this building."

"What is this place?"

"It's called the Johnson Ferry House. My dad said it was an old farmhouse and an inn back in the 1700s. Some guy named Johnson had a big farm and ran a ferry across the river. During the Revolutionary War, some other people ran the ferry and the inn."

Kay nodded. "That's neat."

"My dad said they think George Washington used this house when his army crossed the river to fight the British."

"Have you ever been up here?"

Anna looked back over her shoulder, her mouth drawn tight. "Once with Dad a long time ago."

"It's really hot up here." Kay stepped to a small window, lifted it, and pushed open the shutters.

The land fell away from the house, sloping to River Road, the canal, and the Delaware River. Laser-like rays of summer sun bathed the tops of the trees and glistened on some of the shiniest leaves. The grass in the open areas shone bright emerald.

Kay craned her neck to see over the trees to the river. "Is that the bridge we were on?"

"Yeah, that's the one. It goes over to Pennsylvania."

Kay focused on the bridge. "From here, it looks flimsy with all those metal things crisscrossing the sides and on top."

Buddy squeezed between the girls. "It's safe. We've crossed it a lot."

"We walked across once, Buddy. You got scared the time Mom and Dad went with us." Anna turned toward Kay and shrugged. "He was afraid the bridge wouldn't hold up. It is sort of creepy. I was even nervous that time. Dad says it's perfectly safe."

Buddy shook his grass-stained finger at her. "See, you were scared, too."

"Listen," Anna said, holding up her hand.

Buddy picked at a small piece of skin hanging from his knee. He made squeaky grunts each time he pulled on it.

Anna poked Buddy. "Shhh. Be quiet."

"I can't help it. It hurts."

"I hear a truck or something," Anna said. "It's getting louder. I hope it's not the worker coming back."

The rumble of the engine got closer and steadier. Next they heard the sound of a car door opening and closing.

"We've got to go. If my dad finds out we've been in here, I'm done. I'll be grounded forever."

Buddy moaned and came up on one knee.

A man walked into the house, letting the door slam behind him.

Anna whispered, "Get down."

The three lay on the floor near the top of the stairs and watched.

A man wearing paint-spattered jeans, a stained T-shirt, and a blue cap with a yellow bill stood in front of the fireplace. Reaching into a plastic bag, he took out a can of soda and a sandwich. He chomped on the sandwich. Pieces of lettuce fell out with each bite. Wiping the mayonnaise from the corners of his mouth, he gripped the can and guzzled.

Kay took in a deep breath and checked the time on her phone.

The man finished the meal in less than five minutes and went to the fireplace. He grabbed a hammer and pecked at the bricks.

Anna tapped Kay and Buddy on the shoulder. She put her index finger to her lips and made an up and down motion with her right hand, palm down. All three lay on the floor, watching the man.

Another five minutes passed.

Buddy fanned his face with his hand, glared at Kay, and mouthed, "It's hot in here."

Kay waved her hand across his head in a weak, fanning motion. Buddy threw her arm back.

Tearing at the loose fireplace bricks, the worker dragged out several that stuck together and fell in a clump on the hearth. The crashing startled the three trespassers.

Anna gritted her teeth and shook her head at Kay.

The man tore away more of the fireplace and reached into the hole left by the missing bricks. He pulled his hand back and shook off the bits of cement. Rifling through his toolbox, he picked out a bigger hammer and a large chisel.

Kay winced at every ping of the hammer striking the chisel. She eased her phone out of her capris and showed Anna the time.

The pings soon gave way to loud bangs as the worker struck the bricks directly with the hammer. Grappling with both hands, he tore away the debris and brought out a gray tube.

Buddy squirmed, dragged the toe of his shoe across the rough planks of the floor, and whispered to his sister, "I have to go to the bathroom."

The worker stopped. Holding the tube, he jerked his head to the left and right.

Kay's heart pounded.

Anna's eyes grew big. She patted Buddy's arm.

The man brought his attention back to the object. He felt inside the tube and pulled out a piece of paper. Laying the rolled-up paper on the floor, he revealed portions as his hand flattened the document. He shouted, "I don't believe this! What luck!" He put the document back into the tube, shoved it under a blue tarpaulin, and returned to repairing the fireplace.

Five minutes passed. More banging and chipping.

Kay leaned close to Anna's ear. "I'm going to say something. We could be here for hours."

The noise of the workman masked the sound of the three pulling back from their vantage point.

Buddy touched his sister's arm and muffled his voice with his hand. "I have to go to the bathroom bad, and it's really hot in here."

Anna shrugged, tapped Kay on the arm, and pointed at Buddy.

Kay eased up on one knee. Before she could speak, the man dropped his hammer, took off his work gloves, and headed out the door.

A few seconds later. *Squeak! Bang!*

Kay grabbed Buddy's arm. "It's the portable toilet. I heard the door open and shut. Let's go!"

Buddy jumped up. Kay led the way. Anna followed, stumbling behind the other two. Kay stopped at the foot of the stairs.

Anna groaned. "My leg's asleep."

"You go ahead, Buddy. I'll help Anna. We'll catch up."

Buddy went out the side door to the bikes. Anna held on to Kay's arm till she got to the door. She left Kay and limped outside.

Kay picked her way around debris and tools and went to the tarp. She whipped it up. Dust flew. Coughing, she picked up the tube and ran outside. How would she pedal and hold this heavy container? The water-bottle holder on the bike! She snapped the tube into the bracket on the bike frame.

Anna looked back at Kay. "Are you crazy? What are you doing?"

Kay pushed off on her bike. "Go! Don't worry about it."

Squeak! Bang! Kay twisted in the direction of the noise. She glimpsed someone standing at the corner of the ferry house. She whipped her head back to the front. Her bike wobbled, veered off the road, and bumped back onto the pavement. Standing on the pedals, Kay pumped her legs. She caught up with Anna, who had stopped under a large oak tree by the road. "Where's Buddy?"

Emerging from the bushes, Buddy stood his bike upright. "I told you I had to go bad."

Anna scowled at Kay. "Why did you take that thing?"

"It's not his. Doesn't it belong to the park?"

"I don't care who it belongs to. I don't want to get in trouble with my dad. You knew we weren't supposed to go in the house!"

Kay threw her hands up. "Who's going to find out?"

"You don't care who you get in trouble. Now I know why your friends from Florida haven't called or texted you."

CHAPTER SEVEN

"**A**re you here?"

"Yes, Mom!" Leaving the bedroom door cracked, Kay sat at her desk, the container in front of her. She opened the bottom drawer and took out a battered wooden box covered with stickers and words written with permanent markers and crayons. She placed her contraband inside and covered it with old school papers and drawings. Since preschool, this was her safe—her hiding place for special things. Occasionally Kay would make an attempt to clean out the box. She usually spent more time reminiscing and got rid of very little.

Her mom knocked on the door and pushed it open.

Kay gently closed the lid and leaned on the box with both arms.

Her mom said, "I waited on lunch for you. There's a sandwich in the fridge."

"Thanks. I'll eat in a minute."

"Please clean up after you eat and turn on the dishwasher. I'm going to the mall. I'll be back by four. Please stay home."

"I'll be here when you get home."

"Stay home!"

"I will. Don't worry."

Kay stood near her bedroom window and listened. Her mother closed the back door and started the car seconds later. When the rumble of the car's engine faded, Kay opened the box and stared at the tube. She recalled Anna's comments about her friends.

"Maybe she's right." She closed the box and sat back in the chair. "Do I treat my friends like that?" Kay closed her eyes, thinking about her life in Tallahassee. Small tears trickled down her cheek. She wiped them away with both hands and leaned forward.

"Let's see what I have here that my friend Anna thinks may get her in trouble. Hmmm…my friend. I wonder."

Kay inspected the container, probing with her fingers trying to remove the document. No success. She snapped her fingers. "Tweezers." Returning from the bathroom, she plucked the paper from the tube and unrolled it. "Don't want to rip the paper. I'll bet this is worth a lot of money."

Holding the document under her desk lamp, Kay struggled to read the handwriting. "This is a letter to Colonel Johann Rall, whoever he is. And here's the date, December 22, 1776."

Kay opened her laptop, searched the Internet, and read one of the entries: "On the night of December 25 and 26, 1776, General George Washington crossed the Delaware River at Johnson's Ferry with his troops to attack the Hessian regiments."

"The Johnson Ferry House! Where I picked up the tube!"

Kay remembered very little of this from American history. She flipped her hair and tucked it behind her ears. What was this all about? Why would something like this be stuck in a fireplace? Maybe Anna's dad had some books that would tell her something about the letter and what it would be worth. Kay put the document back in the tube, grabbed her cell phone, and touched Anna's number.

"Buddy? Where's your sister?"

"She's in the bathroom. I picked up her phone."

"Tell her to call me when she gets out."

"She's going to be a while. She's taking a shower and washing her hair, and it takes her forever."

"Please tell her to call."

Kay placed the phone in her pocket. Her stomach growled. Remembering the food in the fridge, she went downstairs. She took the sandwich and sat in the family room, absorbed in a reality TV show on the DVR. Her phone rang. "Anna?"

"No. This is your mother."

"Oops, I thought you were Anna."

"I'm going to be a little longer. I should be back by five. Would you please put the chicken in the oven around four-thirty? It's in the fridge wrapped in foil and ready to cook. Set the oven at four hundred and the timer for an hour. Can you do that for me?"

Kay rolled her eyes. "Yes, Mother, I can do that."

When her mom ended the call, Kay hit Anna's number. She waited a few minutes and tried again. No answer. She left a voice mail: "Anna, I'm coming over."

Kay went to her room, picked up the tube, and placed it in a plastic bag. She grabbed her bike helmet and dashed out of the house.

Riding by the convenience store near the bridge, Kay braked into the parking lot and walked her bike between a brown van and a red pickup. Kay leaned her bike against the wall and entered the store carrying the bag. She came out holding a cup with a straw and pushed off on her bike with the tube safely nestled back in the bottle holder.

The whirring rotating bike chain and the humming tires on the pavement sounded like buzzing insects on this warm summer day. The bike sounds faded, overtaken by the low screams of a straining car engine. Kay eased her head around to her left. A brown van approached. Inching closer to the shoulder, the van accelerated and slowed as it pulled even.

Through the open passenger window, Kay had a clear view of the driver. He wore a blue cap with a yellow bill. The same cap worn by the man in the ferry house. Her heart leaped. The van accelerated. Kay veered into the loose dirt and gravel on the shoulder. The bike wobbled, skidded, and fell over in the grass. The plastic bag with the tube rested a few feet beyond. Soda dribbled down Kay's face and onto her tank top. "Yuck." She yanked the smashed cup from beneath her leg and threw it.

A jogger ran from across the street and knelt beside Kay. "What happened?"

"I'm not sure. I got too close to the shoulder and slid in the gravel."

The woman surveyed Kay and brushed back the unlucky cyclist's hair. "Did that van force you off the road? He was awfully close."

"Maybe he was close or I was too far in the lane." Kay remembered the blue cap and the yellow bill. Her heart raced again. She examined her hands, which were streaked with grass stains, and brushed at the scrapes on her knees.

The woman held Kay's trembling hands. "Are you hurt?"

"No. I'm OK. My friend's house isn't too far. I'm on my way there."

Her legs rubbery, Kay tried to stand. The woman placed her hand under Kay's arm to steady her and helped Kay retrieve the bike. Except for some dirt packed in the pedals, the bicycle had fared well in the spill.

The woman picked up the bag with the container. "This is heavy for such a small package."

Kay smiled at the woman and took the bag. She placed it in the bottle holder. "Thanks for helping me." She walked the bike up the grassy hill to the road, adjusted her helmet, and mounted the bike. "My phone!" It was in her pocket when she crashed. She pulled it out, played with the ringer setting, and slid it back in her capris.

The woman waited for Kay to begin pedaling. "Are you sure you can ride?"

"Yes. I'll be OK."

Kay pedaled slowly and winced at the pain from the scrapes. Her mind raced, recalling the memories of recent bike incidents. This one would surely bring questions. She experienced another moment of panic—how to explain *this* to her parents.

CHAPTER EIGHT

"**W**hat happened to you?" Anna pointed at Kay's stained tank top and the scratches on her legs.

"Is your mom home?"

"No. She took Buddy to swim at the pool. What did you do to your knees? Did you fall off—"

"Let's go to your room." Kay rushed up the stairs, skipping steps.

Anna ran up behind her. "Tell me what's—"

"Shhh." Kay nudged Anna into the bedroom. "Close the door, and lock it." Kay plopped onto the edge of the bed and took several deep breaths. "I think the man with the duck's cap may have tried to run me off the road."

"*What?* What are you talking about?"

"The man with the duck's cap."

"The duck's cap? You're not making sense. You fell off your bike, didn't you? You must've hit your head."

"The man at the ferry house. He had a blue cap with a yellow bill. We were upstairs and saw him. He looked like a duck waddling around."

"Stop. Let's start over." Anna's mouth fell open.

Kay removed the container from the plastic bag and laid the heavy tube on the bed.

"I knew it!" Anna's eyes widened. "He saw us take the tube, and he wants it back."

"The man couldn't have seen us, or he would've come after us. He wasn't going to tell anyone because he doesn't want anybody to know about it."

"How did he know you were coming to my house?"

"I don't know." Kay touched the scrapes on her leg. "Wait a minute. The van he drove. It was parked at the store where I stopped to buy a drink."

"Do you think he waited for you?"

"No. It had to be luck. He must've seen me when I left the store."

"When he drove up beside you on the road, do you think he recognized you?"

Kay ran her fingers through her hair and frowned. "I don't know. Maybe he tried to get a look at me—you know, a girl on a bike—and he got too close."

"This is too much." Anna swallowed hard and put her hands on top of her head, fingers clasped. "What if he finds out where you live, or where I live and—"

"And what?" Kay asked. "If we give this thing to the park visitor center, he won't have a reason to bother us."

"And I'll be grounded for a year when we explain how we got it." Anna shook her head. "You know we weren't supposed to be in the construction areas in the park. And with the burglary at the visitor center, I'm sure this would not make my dad happy. I don't like this."

"Then let's find out if this is really important. If it is, everyone will be glad we found it when we turn it in. Even if we say we found it in the park, people will be so pleased that they'll forget about how we got it."

Anna's eyes widened. "What about the man at the ferry house?"

"We don't know if he knows we have the tube. Besides, he won't say anything. He was going to keep it for himself."

Anna put her hands on her hips. "How do you know that?"

"Why do you think he tried to hide it?"

"You're right. But I'm still scared. He did try to run you off the road, right?"

Kay wished she hadn't revealed so much about the incident. Somehow she needed to calm Anna. "He slowed down and drove right beside me. I saw his cap, and I panicked."

"Which is it? Did he try to run you off the road, or did you panic?"

"I…let's see…I…Let's get this thing out of the tube. It could be really valuable. Since your dad is the Washington Crossing head guy, maybe he has some books that could help us. That's why I came over here." Kay grinned and held up the heavy tube.

Anna cocked her head to one side and glared at Kay. She snatched the bag from Kay's hand, looked in the tube, and probed with her fingers.

"I tried that," Kay said. "Get some tweezers. And be careful, this thing is very old. The paper might tear."

Anna returned from the bathroom, gripped the document with the tweezers, and removed it from the protective tube.

"Anna!" Buddy tugged at the handle of the locked door. "I jumped off the high dive. Are you in there? I saw Kay's bike out front."

"Mom's home. Here, hide this." Anna let go of the paper, leaving it halfway out of the tube, and handed the tube to Kay.

Kay shoved the heavy container in the plastic bag, bent down, and gently slid the package under the bed.

Anna unlocked the door and jerked it open.

Buddy stumbled, almost falling into the room. "I jumped off the high dive today. I wasn't scared either." He twisted from side to side, glaring at each girl. "What are you two doing?"

Kay sat on the bed. "Nothing. We were talking."

Buddy leaned forward and reached out his hand to touch the scrapes on Kay's legs. "What happened to you?"

Kay slid over and drew her legs close. "I fell off my bike."

"Yeah? Like me, huh."

"That's right. I hit some gravel on the edge of the road and slid down a bank."

Buddy gritted his teeth and grimaced. "Does it hurt?"

"Not now."

Anna waved at Buddy. "We were having some *girl* talk. How about leaving?"

"But I wanted to tell you about my high dive."

Anna grabbed his shoulder, spun him, and tried to scoot him out the door. "That's great, Buddy. It took me a long time to get the nerve to jump off that dive."

Kay patted him on the shoulder. "That's terrific, Buddy."

"What's this?" The boy freed himself from his sister's grip. He spotted the edge of the container exposed in the plastic bag.

Kay kicked at the tube to push it farther under the bed.

Buddy reached for the bag. Kay grabbed for it, but he was closer and picked it up.

"It's that thing you took from the park!"

Anna put her finger to her lips and stuck her face close to Buddy's. "Shhh. Not so loud."

Buddy raised his shoulders and whispered, "What are you doing?"

Kay reached for the bag. "Lock the door." She placed the tube on Anna's desk and pulled on the paper.

Anna put her hands at the mouth of the tube and caught the other end of the document when it emerged.

"Let me see." Buddy reached for the document.

Anna pushed him back. "Don't touch it."

Kay patted Buddy on the arm, stopping him from pulling on the paper. "You can see it. It's delicate. We don't want to tear it."

Kay cleared an area on the desk and rolled out the mysterious document. "Buddy, put your hand here. Anna, you hold it in this spot."

The trio stared at the document.

Buddy squinted and leaned in. "What's it say?"

Kay said, "We don't know yet. But the date on the letter means it was written around the time Washington crossed the Delaware."

"Must be a letter to somebody," Buddy said.

Anna stepped back and tapped her brother on the shoulder. "Hel-lo, Buddy. Of course it's a letter."

Kay shook her head. "Come on, you two. Focus."

Buddy pointed at some words. "Who's it from? George Washington?"

Kay flattened an area of the letter. "Maybe. If it's not him, let's see if we can figure out who wrote it."

Anna pushed Buddy aside for a clear view of the document. When Buddy fell away, his end of the document curled over onto Anna's hand.

"Be careful." Kay slid her hand across the paper and unrolled it. "This thing could be worth a lot of money."

Buddy wedged himself between Anna and Kay. "How do you know that?"

Anna again brushed her brother aside. "She's right. I'll bet it's worth a lot. It looks like some of the things that were stolen from the visitor-center museum."

The letter slipped from beneath Kay's fingers and curled up on one corner. "Somebody thinks these things are worth something, or else why would they take a chance on stealing them?"

Buddy again muscled his way between the two girls. "I want to know what it says."

"We're trying to read it, if you don't mind." Anna pushed Buddy's hand aside and ran her hand to the bottom of the letter.

Buddy pushed back. "Watch it."

Kay tapped the brother and sister on the shoulders. "Keep it down, will you?"

Anna squinted. "I was trying to see if anybody signed the letter."

Kay helped her flatten the bottom right portion. "The signature's smudged. Water or something dripped on it."

Buddy rubbed his hand over his buzz cut. "Why did somebody write a letter and hide it?"

"Who knows?" Kay shrugged and put her face close to the paper. "The whole thing's hard to read. This word must be 'preparation.'"

Anna ran her finger along a line of words. "And this sentence is about a meeting place."

The girls pieced together some of the message, sharing each other's discoveries. Buddy wedged his head between them.

Kay stepped back, letting her side of the letter roll up.

Anna said, "Let me get some of Dad's books. He's got a bunch on George Washington and the Revolutionary War." She left and returned with three volumes.

Kay opened the index of a large book, ran her finger to an item, and flipped to one of the book's inside pages. "Here's an interesting article. It explains why we see ice on the river in that painting of

Washington crossing the Delaware. Listen to this: 'The height of the Little Ice Age is generally dated as 1650 to 1850 A.D. The American Revolutionary Army, under General George Washington, shivered at Valley Forge in the winter of 1777 and 1778, and New York harbor was frozen in the winter of 1780.'"

Kay flipped more pages, stopped, and read: "Washington and the army were staying immediately across the river in Pennsylvania in late 1776."

Anna located an entry and scanned the page. "It says here that morale was low in the Continental Army and that General Washington was having a difficult time keeping many of the volunteers from leaving."

"What's morale?"

"It's the way you feel, Buddy," Anna said. "You know, basically happy or sad."

Kay opened another history book. "Here's something about the morale of the army in this book, and it talks about Washington crossing the river."

Buddy sat on the bed next to Kay, bumping her. "Read it."

"I will. Not so close, will you? 'Morale in the army was low, so George Washington—commander in chief of the Continental Army—devised a plan to cross the Delaware River on the night of December 25 and 26 and surround the Hessian garrison.'"

Buddy angled his head at the letter. "What's a Hessian?"

Kay went to the index again and found a listing for "Hessian." She opened a page, and read: "It says here the Hessians were Germans hired by the British to help fight the Americans."

Buddy put his elbows on the desk. "Why did they do that? Didn't they have their own guys?"

"This explains it." Anna read a passage: "'The German soldiers hired by the British received wages, but the prince of their respective German states received most of the funds. Most soldiers were from the Hesse region in Germany. Britain found it easier to borrow money to pay for their service than to recruit its own soldiers.'"

"Here's something about the crossing of the Delaware." Kay lifted the book, cradled it on one arm, and read: "'The crossing proved dangerous because of the icy river and the severe weather. Two detachments were unable to cross the river, leaving Washington with 2,400 men for the assault. The army marched nine miles south to Trenton. Assuming they were safe from the American army, the Hessians dropped their guard, having no long-distance outposts or patrols. Washington's forces caught the Hessians off guard, and after a short but fierce resistance, most of the German soldiers surrendered. Almost two-thirds of the 1,500-man garrison was captured, and only a few troops escaped. Despite the battle's small numbers, the American victory inspired rebels in the colonies. With the success of the revolution in doubt a week earlier, the army had seemed on the verge of collapse. The dramatic victory inspired soldiers to serve longer and attracted new recruits to the ranks.'"

Kay closed the book. "I don't think these are much help. Besides, there's too much to go through. Lots of history, but nothing about this letter or any other historic documents."

Anna scanned the letter. "He's writing to someone with a German name—a Colonel John Rall? No, That's Johann."

Kay stepped back. "I read about him when I first did a search. He's not just *someone*. He was the leader of the Hessian troops in Trenton."

The cordless phone rang. All three jumped. By the time Anna reached for it, the ringing stopped. "My mom must've answered it." She returned to the open page. "Why is someone writing a letter to the enemy?"

Kay scratched her head. "I'm not sure—"

"Anna! Buddy!"

Buddy ran to the door. "It's my mom."

Anna cut him off and cracked open the door. "We're up here!"

"Is Kay with you?"

"Yes!"

"Her mother said for her to come home. She wasn't supposed to leave the house. I think she's upset."

Kay glanced at her phone; it was 4:46. "I had my phone on silent! I must've changed it by accident when I checked it after the bike crash!" She saw a missed call from her mom, threw her head back, and closed her eyes.

Buddy smirked. "Bus-ted."

"Stop it, Buddy!" Anna poked him with her finger and yelled, "Tell her mother she's on her way." She stared at Kay. "What do we do about the letter?"

Kay rolled it up and shoved it back in the tube. "Keep it here. I'll call you tonight."

Anna's voice quivered. She grabbed Kay's arm. "Then what'll we do? I don't want my dad to find out. I already got in trouble just before school was out. It was bad enough that I didn't take the bus home and then the…the…the police…forget it; you wouldn't understand. Believe me, I can't get into any more trouble."

Kay squeezed her friend's hand. "I won't get you in any more trouble, I promise. For now, please hide the letter, and I'll think about what to do later."

Riding back to her house, Kay thought about Anna, who had started to confess to something. Kay herself had plenty of confessions to make. She experienced being seriously grounded at least five times over her brief life span. One of the more serious incidents occurred a few weeks before the move to New Jersey.

Without telling her mom, Kay had ridden with a group of girls to the mall four miles from her house. One of the friends had veered into traffic, and a car brushed by her causing her to crash. The young girl had a broken wrist and some cuts and bruises. The incident resulted in extreme guilt for Kay—and fear, anger, and disappointment from her parents.

The more Kay recalled the Tallahassee episode, the more she regretted taking the tube with the letter from the ferry house. Her parents could never know about the letter and the bike spill on River Road. The grounding would be the worst ever. But now Kay had a greater fear. She had promised Anna that they wouldn't get in trouble with the letter—a letter that maybe someone else desperately wanted.

CHAPTER NINE

Kay raced through the kitchen, expecting the worst.

"Just a minute, young lady."

She stopped, hesitated, and faced her mother.

"Didn't I ask you to stay home? You didn't even leave me a note. It must've sounded strange to Anna's mom, me calling to ask if my daughter was at her house. And why didn't you answer your phone?"

"I...I think I had it on silent by accident."

"On silent! Kay, that's the main reason we got you the phone so we can stay in touch. It's for your safety."

Kay drew her shoulders up and winced. "Sorry, Mom."

Her mom scowled and shook her head. "You're thirteen years old—soon to be fourteen. I need to be able to trust you. I should ground you for a week."

Kay knew her mom. She would come around, but her mom needed time to cool off.

"What happened to your knees? And your top is stained. Did you fall off your bike?"

Kay ran through the possible answers. If she gave the wrong one, her mom would surely ground her. The Tallahassee incident flashed through her mind. "We were...riding...riding our bikes around the yard, kind of in a race, and I slid on some wet grass."

"See. That's why I worry. Suppose you were hurt badly or hit your head."

Kay shuddered. The door incident at the park visitor center and the overnight stay in the hospital flooded her thoughts. She gave her mother a hug. "I didn't mean to make you worry."

The pulsating veins in her mom's neck disappeared. She dropped the dishtowel on the counter. "I know that, but you did." She hugged Kay. "I love you, but you're giving me more gray hair."

Kay smiled and touched her mom's arm. "I know. I'm sorry. I love you, too. I'll go change clothes and come back down to help you with dinner."

"Thanks. That would be nice."

Kay passed through the dining room.

Opening the dishwasher, her mom called out, "No going online tonight."

Kay walked toward the stairs, never looking back. Her cell phone rang as she stepped into the bedroom. It was Anna.

"Are you in trouble?"

"A little. Mom was mad and I came close to being grounded. So far, all she said was that I can't go online tonight."

"At least she didn't take away your phone."

"Not yet. I have to play this cool. My dad could make things worse. I'm on shaky ground with my parents. I didn't tell you this, but I pulled a good one a few weeks before we left Florida."

Kay told Anna about the Tallahassee bike incident. "Now that I've had another episode with my bike—probably caused by me taking the letter—I have a good reason to keep this whole thing from my parents, too. I shouldn't have made you go into the ferry house."

Anna sighed. "I agreed to go in."

Kay bit her lip and ran her fingers through her hair. "Are you still worried that your father will find out about us going in the house and the letter?"

"It's not just the letter. I…"

Kay coughed and reached for her water bottle.

Anna said, "There's something I need to tell you."

Kay heard Anna's deep breathing.

"I was arrested in May by the police here in the township."

Kay's mouth dropped open. She sat up, pushed herself against the headboard, and shifted the phone to her right ear.

Anna continued, "I know it sounds bad. I'm not a criminal, but I did get into some trouble—mostly with my parents. I suppose I was in the wrong place at the wrong time. Or maybe it was being with the wrong people."

"What happened?"

"On the last day of school this year, a girlfriend of mine, Abby, and her boyfriend, Tommy, wanted me to ride home with them instead of taking the bus. Tommy had just gotten his driver's license. His older brother was home from college and had let Tommy drive his convertible to school. Abby said they would take me straight home. When we got in the car, Tommy asked me if I wanted to ride up River Road to Lambertville and back with them. It was a nice spring day, so I said, 'Why not.'"

Kay had not anticipated this from Anna. Her eyes widened. "Arrested? Why were you arrested?"

"We were almost back to my friend's house, and Tommy drove a little fast. The Hopewell police stopped us."

Kay jumped in. "Tommy got a ticket for speeding, and your parents got mad because you didn't ride the bus. That doesn't seem like such a big deal."

"That's only part of it. The police officer made Tommy open the trunk of the car, and there were some empty beer cans inside."

"Whoa, what happened?"

"He told the police officer that the beer cans weren't his. He showed the officer the registration and everything, but the officer got tough with Tommy. The officer said there had been a couple of incidents of teenagers drinking and driving in the past few months. Two kids were killed in a wreck in North Jersey in May. The driver was legally drunk. He was seventeen."

"That's sad. I don't like to hear those stories. What happened to you?"

"The police officer made us get into the patrol car, and he took us to the police station. I think he was trying to scare us, because Tommy only got a warning."

"He was lucky."

"Lucky, yes, but things got worse."

"Worse?"

"Oh, yes—they called our parents."

"Ouch."

"Yeah, ouch is right. On top of all this, one of the police officers knew my dad. They went to high school together and played on the basketball team. It was very embarrassing when my parents came to get me."

Kay was speechless. She'd never been in a situation like that with *her* parents. Her voice softened. "I understand. But I don't think you did anything so wrong by riding in your friend's car."

"I didn't think it was that serious either. Too bad my parents had a different opinion."

Kay shook her head. "Parents can be really tough."

"That's in the past now. What bothers me more is this letter thing. Now that someone has tried to run you off the road to get it, this whole mess is getting worse. It would break my dad's heart for him to know I disobeyed him again—and so soon—and my mom will be very disappointed. On top of being yelled at, my parents said they would make me change schools and go to St. Albans and leave all my friends at River High."

"Were they serious?"

"Very. They didn't like Abby and some of the other girls in our group at school. Some of them have steady boyfriends, and my parents say I'm too young to date and that Abby's not a good influence." Anna's voice rose. "We *have* to get rid of this letter, and quick."

"I'll think of something," Kay said. "Thanks for telling me all this. Let's talk tomorrow."

• • •

The conversation over dinner that evening at the Telfair house began with an innocent question from Kay's father, but Kay knew where it would lead.

"What've you been up to today?"

Mom jumped in. "Your daughter was very busy. I asked her to stay home and do a few things for me while I went shopping. But she went over to Anna's house. One of those chores was to put the chicken in the oven. That's the reason we're eating late."

Kay waited for the whole story to unfold. She had no defense—at least not one she wanted to reveal.

"She, Anna, and Buddy were racing on their bikes, and Kay fell off and scraped her—"

"But not bad," Kay said. "It was nothing."

Kay's mom cleared her throat. "She only scraped her knees, but she could've been hurt badly."

Her dad looked at Kay. "Is that right?"

"That's about it." Kay waited for her dad to react. If he backed her mom, that would ensure Kay would be grounded.

"Be careful," he said. "I'd hate for you to have to spend another summer day in the hospital."

"I'll be careful. I promise." Kay detected an opening. "Say, Dad, may I go online tonight? Just for a few minutes? I want to research some history stuff about Washington Crossing."

Her mom huffed and glared at her husband. "I told her she couldn't go online."

Kay's dad picked up the carving knife and sliced into the roasted chicken. "Why the sudden interest in Washington Crossing?"

"Anna's gotten me interested. She knows a lot about the history of this area." Kay tried one more ploy. "And maybe it'll help me to think of this place as our. . .as *my* new home."

Dad smiled. "What do you say, Mom?"

Her mom shook her head and sighed. "I give up."

CHAPTER TEN

Kay opened the laptop. She typed "historic letters about Washington Crossing" into the search box and clicked on four websites. None of them was what she wanted. She went to the kitchen for a soda and returned to the bedroom.

"Any luck?" Dad sat in front of Kay's computer.

In mid swallow, Kay almost choked. "Not much. I've checked out a few sites." She stood next to her dad and placed the glass on the desk.

Her dad gripped the mouse. The cursor zigzagged across the screen. "Here's some interesting stuff about the ferry landing where Washington crossed the Delaware. It was called Johnson's Ferry on the New Jersey side and McConkey's Ferry on the Penn side. There's a house at the Park called the Johnson Ferry House. It was used by Washington's troops during the Battle of Trenton."

Kay coughed, almost sending soda out her nose. "That's interesting. I—that is, Buddy, Anna, and me—we saw the house when we went for a ride in the park."

"Anna and *I*—and who's Buddy?"

"Oops. *Anna and I.* Buddy is Anna's little brother."

"Here's something interesting." He scrolled down the page. "One of Washington's officers wrote about the crossing after the war. It looks like Washington crossed over ahead of some his troops and watched the crossing while sitting on a box that was an old beehive. Listen to this: 'Men were stationed in the bows of the boats with boat hooks to keep off the cakes of ice, and the roar of the waters and the crash of the ice almost drowned the words of command.'" He chuckled. "I can't wait till our first winter here. It's hard to imagine the Delaware full of ice."

He glanced at his daughter. "That was a little boring, wasn't it?"

"No, no, that was interesting."

He kissed her on the cheek. "That's enough for tonight. Thanks for letting me butt into your research."

Kay moved in front of the computer. "Anytime, Dad."

Kay yawned and stretched. Reaching down with her right hand, she touched the scrapes on her knees. She blinked and shook her head to get rid of the memories and then started another search. Cupping her hand around the mouse, she reached for the glass of soda. A site called Historical Doc Search popped up. She read the description: "A quick and easy way to research your historical documents and determine their value."

Kay clicked on the name, and the browser symbol started spinning. A message from Anna popped up on Kay's phone. "Did you get in trouble?"

Kay answered: "I've been looking for some information on the letter. I'll be done in about ten minutes. I'll call you."

The web page loaded, showing another list of references. One caught her attention: Historical Research, Inc., Princeton, New Jersey. The description read: "Old documents to sell? Let us help you. No charge for inquiries."

Princeton. Now she was getting somewhere. A company so close to the park should be able to help. She clicked the e-mail link. How to phrase her questions about the letter? What if her dad saw the e-mails?

Kay exited her e-mail and set up a free, new account with the user name "history1776me." She clicked on the Historical Research page and typed: "I am a student in summer school taking a history class, and we are studying the Revolutionary War…"

Kay paused and deleted the lines. Her fingers tapped the keys: "I have a letter from the Revolutionary War written by someone in Washington's army about the time of the Battle of Trenton. The date on the letter is December 22, 1776. I am interested in selling it."

She sent the e-mail and searched again. Another website, History Collectors, sparked her interest. The site showed a post office box in Trenton. She sent the same message e-mailed to Historical Research. It asked for her name and address. "I'm not giving them my name. No way."

She reached for her cell phone. "Buddy, where's Anna?"

"She's helping Mom. Her phone was ringing, and I answered it."

"Tell her I called and to call me tomorrow, but not before eight."

"Are you in trouble?"

"Just tell Anna to call me tomorrow."

Kay thought about Buddy's question. She promised Anna they wouldn't get in trouble. She had to keep that promise.

CHAPTER ELEVEN

"That sound. What's that sound?" Kay mumbled and shielded her eyes. She rolled over, grabbed the cell phone, and hit the speaker icon.

Anna's voice crackled. "What did your parents say?"

Kay sat up in bed and looked at the time: 7:23.

"Hel-lo, Kay!"

"I'm here, I'm awake—I think. You're up early."

"Mom left to go into the city with my aunt. She woke me before she left. Buddy didn't want to go, and now I have to babysit."

"I told Buddy to tell you to call me after eight."

"At least he told me you called. What happened when your dad got home?"

Kay sat up and shook her head, trying to think. "Not much. I'm still on my mom's bad list, but Dad's on my side. It takes a lot to get him angry, but if I do get him mad at me, look out. I'd be grounded for sure. I'm OK for now." Kay slid out of the bed and turned on the computer. "I found these two websites for buying and selling historical artifacts and sent an e-mail asking about our letter."

"You did *what?* It's bad enough we, well, you stole the—"

"We—or I—didn't *steal* anything. We *found* it. And I didn't give any details. I asked about how much a letter from the Revolutionary War would be worth."

"I think we should give the letter to somebody," Anna said. "If my dad finds out, that'll be the end of my summer—and maybe my life."

"Anna, that somebody should be your dad."

"He'll kill me if we do that."

"Not if we tell him in the right way. I think the best way to do that is to start off with how valuable this letter is. Your dad will be so happy we found it, he'll forget about how we got it. Plus, with the other stuff being stolen from the park, this may make him feel better about all that."

"Do you believe that?"

"If you want, we could go to him right now and say we were in the construction area where we weren't supposed to be, and we saw this man find this container with a letter, but he didn't know we saw him. And when he went to the bathroom, we left and took the container and—"

"I get the point. What about the man trying to run you off the road?"

"I don't think he'll do anything. He only wanted to see who I was."

"That means he knows we have the letter. What if he tries to get it back or tells my father we were in the construction area?"

Kay stared at the phone. She took a deep breath, waved the device in the air, and put it back to her ear. "Anna, believe me, the man won't do anything. He wanted to hide the container and wasn't going to tell anyone, especially your dad."

"When will you know what it's worth?"

"I sent the e-mail last night. Maybe I'll hear back today. I haven't logged on to check my mail. I created another e-mail account and didn't set it up on my phone in case my mom checked it. If I don't get a reply today, I'll check on Monday when we get back."

"Back from where?"

"We're going to Rhode Island this weekend to see my grandparents. We'll be back on Monday."

"That means I've got to keep the letter all weekend until you get back?"

"Please do this for me—for us. Hide it. I'll come over when we get home, and by that time, I should know if it's worth anything. After that, we can tell your dad."

"Promise me we'll get rid of it after you find out."

"Don't worry. Nobody knows where the letter is but us: you, me, and Buddy. And make sure Buddy doesn't blab."

"He won't tell. But this whole thing scares me. I wish we—*you*—had never taken the letter."

"To be honest, so do I. But, it's too late to worry about that now."

CHAPTER TWELVE

Kay opened the car door and grabbed her duffle and two pillows from the back. "May I have the back door key, Dad?" Fumbling with the key, she pushed the door open, ran through the kitchen to the stairs and up to her room. She walked over to her computer. Her cell phone rang. She stared at the screen. "Anna. I can't talk to her now."

Kay pored over her e-mails. Among a dozen, one was from Anna, asking her to call. Replies from websites where she had sent her inquiries also popped up. She clicked on the first and read: "Thank you for contacting us. If you have a particular document in mind, please describe it, and I will try to estimate its value. The next step would be a visual appraisal to determine the document's condition. Historical Research, Inc."

Kay hit the reply button, took her fingers from the keyboard, and paused. She opened the second e-mail. The sender also asked for more information. She needed to look at the letter again. Kay started a video chat and leaned in toward the microphone. Anna's face appeared.

"Kay, you won't believe this. They took the tube! But Buddy took the letter out, and they didn't get it. The police were here, and I don't know what to do. I'm scared!"

"Slow down, slow down. What are you talking about? Who did what?"

"I said they *took it*. Somebody broke into the house and stole the tube while we were at the shore on Saturday!"

Her heart pounding, Kay almost stopped breathing. "Did they take anything else?"

"Mom says she thinks they took some cash lying on the kitchen counter."

"Maybe the burglar was after valuables and thought the container was worth something. You did say they didn't get the letter, right?"

"Yes. They didn't take it. Buddy went in my room without my permission and took the letter out. He said he wanted to see it. He couldn't get it back in the tube, so he put it behind my bureau."

"Did you tell the police about it?"

"No. I didn't tell them."

Kay sifted through ideas.

"What are we going do? We need to tell somebody."

"Don't worry. We'll find a way to get rid of the letter, and nobody will know how we got it." Kay sounded confident, but inside she was a bundle of nerves. She had no idea how to get out of this mess, short of being grounded for the rest of her life—or worse. But Anna was easily rattled, and one of them needed to keep a cool head. "First, we have to find out how valuable this letter is. When we know that, we'll figure out what to do next."

"What difference does it make how much it's worth? We've got to get rid of it! Let's throw it in the trash or mail it to my dad's office."

Mailing it. Not a bad idea, but what about the man in the ferry house? If he thought the girls had the letter, how would he know they got rid of it? Kay cleared her head. "Let's mail it, but I still want to find out what this thing is worth."

"Even if it's worth a million dollars, you'll still mail it, right?"

"Of course. But I'm curious. It's got to be worth a lot. Why would whoever broke into the visitor center take only the letters and other things people wrote?"

"Kay, your curiosity has gotten us into enough trouble. Let's forget what it's worth and mail it. Let's take it to the post office tomorrow."

"I will—we will. We'll do it tomorrow. But, since you have the letter, can you read it and send me what it says in an e-mail? Type as much as you can."

"Why?"

"I want to do a little research tonight."

"I don't know why I let you talk me into these things."

A half hour later, Kay opened the e-mails from the two websites she had contacted. She pasted the words Anna sent and wrote: "Here is a sample of the letter. I hope this gives you an idea of what it is about so that you can help me." She did the same for the second e-mail and sat back. Before she closed Anna's e-mail, she read what her friend had copied from the letter. Her jaw dropped. Something didn't fit with what she had read about the Battle of Trenton and Washington's army crossing the Delaware. Maybe this letter was worth more than she imagined.

CHAPTER THIRTEEN

"It's time to get up. Did your hear me?"

Throwing off the covers, Kay groaned and went to the door. "I'm up. What time is it?"

"A little past nine."

"I need to call Anna."

"No phone calls and no going online until you've finished some chores. I need your help this morning." Her mother stuck her head back in the doorway. "And don't go back to bed. I need you."

Kay closed the door, fell on the bed, and buried her head in the pillow. Sixty seconds later, she rolled off the bed onto her knees and shuffled over to the nightstand. She picked up her cell phone. Dead. She ran her hand down behind the nightstand, found the charging cord, and plugged it into the phone.

Spotting the cordless phone on the charger, she raised the handset to her ear.

"I'm on the phone with your grandmother. Remember what I said? No talking on the phone, please—even the home phone—till you've done a few things around here."

"Oops. Sorry."

Kay dressed, went to the kitchen, and opened the refrigerator. Her mom had not grounded her, but Kay needed to be careful.

Her mom clamped her hand over the receiver. "Before you eat, please roll the can to the curb. The trash collector will be coming soon, and we missed the last pickup."

Kay gave the fridge door an extra hard push, and went outside. Pulling the can down the drive, her mind wandered to the letter and the promise she had made to Anna. She walked faster when she heard the low growling of the garbage truck's engine.

Slam, bang, plunk! The truck grabbed and lifted each can with the automatic arm, dumping it in the back and returning it to the curb.

Reaching the sidewalk, Kay wrestled with the container. "There." She gave the can a light kick. Her gaze shifted up the street. "Made it in time."

The popping sound from a straining engine grabbed Kay's attention. She spun around. A van swung wide, braking hard as it approached the trash truck. It drove up behind the truck and then passed slowly. The brown van! Kay turned, and ran right out of her left flip-flop. She picked it up and raced to the back door, peeking around the corner as the van drove slowly by and out of sight.

Kay ran into the house and through the kitchen. She brushed by her mom, still on the phone.

Her mom hung up and followed close behind.

Running up the stairs into her bedroom, Kay sat on the edge of the bed, panting.

Her mom opened the bedroom door. "What's the matter?"

No answer.

"Kay, are you all right?"

"I feel sick." Kay bolted for the bathroom. "I think I'm going to throw up."

Ten minutes later, Kay lay on the bed. Her mom held a damp cloth to Kay's head. "Lie here for a few minutes until you feel better."

Curling up on the bed, Kay wrapped her arms around a pillow and stuffed a larger one under her head.

"I'll check on you later. Rest for a while. Do you want something to drink?"

"No, thanks. I want to be quiet here for a few minutes."

Her mom left the room. Kay sat up, steadied herself with her outstretched arms, and reached for the phone. She brought the phone back to the bed and touched the "talk" button, listening to see if her mother was on the line. She punched in Anna's number. Busy. She tried several more times. Falling back on the bed, she squeezed her pillow, closed her eyes, and fell into a deep sleep.

● ● ●

Kay sat up straight in the middle of the bed. "What time is it?" She stared at her cell phone for a few seconds then grabbed it. That was the irritating noise that woke her from her paralyzing slumber. "Hello?"

"Kay?"

"Anna? I tried to call you. You won't believe what happened."

"What's wrong? What are you talking about?"

"The brown van—it drove by my house this morning."

"You mean the guy at the ferry house?"

"Yep, him."

"What was he doing?"

"I don't know. He was driving by."

Anna took a deep breath. "Did he see you?"

"I don't think so."

"This is scary. Are you coming over? You promised we'd go to the post office and mail the letter."

"Hold on." Kay read the note taped to her doorjamb. "I don't know if I can come to your house. My mom's gone to the doctor. Said she'll be back by two-thirty, and she told me to stay home and rest. I was asleep when she left."

"You promised."

"I know. Let me think. What time is it?"

"Almost noon."

"Did I sleep that long?"

"I don't understand. Why were you asleep? Are you sick?"

"The whole thing with seeing the van made me nauseous. I lay down hoping I would feel better, and I fell asleep. I'll be over later. I need to eat something first."

"You'd better come. You promised."

"I promise." Kay ended the call and lay on the bed, staring at the ceiling. Anna was right. This was getting scary.

CHAPTER FOURTEEN

Anna opened the front door. "It's about time you got here." She grabbed Kay's arm and pulled her into the house.

"Take it easy, will you," Kay said. "I'm not feeling all that great."

Anna folded her arms. "I can't go to the post office with you. My mom's gone food shopping and told me to watch Buddy while she's gone."

"When's she coming back?"

"Maybe an hour, maybe two."

"I can't go either. I'll throw up if I have to ride all the way to the post office in this heat. Anyway, I have to get back home before Mom."

"Why did you come over here if you're sick?"

"I was hoping to convince *you* to go to the post office by yourself."

"I said *I can't*. I'm supposed to watch Buddy."

"I'll take care of your brother."

"My mom will find out, and I'll be in trouble like you."

"How's she going to find out?"

"I don't know, but she will."

Buddy came through the door. "What's going on? You guys playing with the letter again?"

Anna glared at her brother. "Where's Derrick?"

"He had to go."

Kay glanced at Anna and tapped Buddy on the shoulder. "How about you and me playing some video games? Anna's going to the store."

Anna's mouth dropped. She rolled her eyes.

Buddy gazed back and forth between Kay and Anna. He focused on his sister. "Mom said you were supposed to stay here with me, and she told me to tell you not to go off on your bike with Kay."

Anna shrugged.

Kay drew her mouth up to one side, waggled her head, and sneered at Buddy.

Anna fell back on the bed. "What are we going to do?"

"I don't know. But I do know I'd better start for home. My mom will be back soon. She's expecting me to be at home resting, and I don't want to answer any questions about why I wasn't feeling so good."

"You're pressing your luck."

"I know, bad judgment. Anyway, if I can get home before her, I'm no worse off."

The sound of a vehicle turning into the driveway at the back of the house sent Anna to the window. She opened the shade, craning her neck to see out. "I think Mom's home."

Hearing the sound, Buddy corrected her. "It's Dad."

"He's home early." Anna drew her mouth up to one side and tilted her head. "I wonder what's up."

Buddy ran to the window. "I told you it was Dad."

The whine of another car engine caught Buddy's attention. "Now that's Mom's car."

The trio stared out the window. Anna's dad waited for his wife to get out of her car. The two stood talking.

Anna cracked open the window. Buddy elbowed his way onto the windowsill. "Hey—"

Anna covered his mouth with her hand. "Be quiet. I want to hear what they're saying. Something's going on. Dad doesn't look happy."

Buddy stepped back and brushed her hand away. "I don't like you putting your hand over my mouth."

"Shhh. I won't do it again."

Buddy sulked and stepped back to the window.

Anna's dad laid his briefcase on the hood of the truck. "You're not going to believe this. I'm a suspect in the burglary."

"What? Who says? Why you?"

"The director called and gave me a heads up. He said the FBI has some evidence that might link me to the break-in."

"What evidence?"

"I don't know. The FBI considers me a person of interest. I was so angry and upset, I decided to leave the park early."

Anna's dad retrieved his briefcase and walked with his wife to the back door. Shaking his head, he looked down and said, "I don't believe this."

Anna put her hands on top of her head and brought them down on the back of her neck. "I don't believe it either."

Buddy leaned on the sill. "Why's Dad so sad?"

"He's not sad." Anna put her arm over Buddy's shoulder. "I think he's tired and worried about this whole mess."

Kay stared out the window. Mess. That was a good word to describe everything…a *real big* mess.

CHAPTER FIFTEEN

"**N**o frozen yogurt?" Kay's dad closed the freezer. "I didn't buy any because you said you didn't need any. Your weight, you said."

Her dad raised his hand. "Don't listen to me. What do I know? Let's go to Mario's and get a gelato."

Kay's mom loaded the last plates in the dishwasher. "Are you sure? It's quarter after eight."

"Let's do it. Do you want to go get some gelato, Kay? You didn't eat much dinner."

Kay wiped the place mats and threw the paper towel in the trash. "I'll stay here, and you can bring me back a coffee gelato."

Her mom grabbed her purse hanging from a chair. "Large, medium, or small?"

"Large, of course."

Her dad waved his keys. "We'll be back in a few."

Returning to the family room, Kay sat in a recliner and picked up the remote.

"Kay!"

"Yes, Mom, I hear you."

"Will you take out the garbage in the kitchen, please?" She chuckled. "I'll bring you a gelato if you'll do that."

"Sure." Kay walked back into the kitchen, smiling. "Nice. They offer me a gelato and then make me work for it. It's worth it."

Her dad, car keys in hand, stuck his head back into the kitchen. "And please lock the door when you come back in."

Kay waved and went to the cabinet beneath the sink. Pulling out the sliding trash can, she lifted and cinched the bag. She went outside to the large green container, opened it, and dropped the bag in. "Phew." Kay curled her nose and backed away. The phone in her pocket rang.

"Hi, Anna, what's up?" Kay walked and talked, opening the back door and pushing it closed. She headed through the kitchen, shut off the lights, and went up the stairs to her room.

"Did anybody reply to your e-mails and tell you how much the letter's worth?"

"Not yet."

The girls chatted for fifteen minutes as the sunlight faded and the bedroom darkened. Kay got Anna off the topic of the letter and told her about her life in Tallahassee. "There were lots of lakes in the area where we lived and…I forgot to lock the back door!" She walked out of the bedroom.

"Kay, are you there?"

Kay put the phone to her ear. "I have to go do something. I'll call you back." Sliding the phone into her pocket, she walked past her parents' room, searching for the light switch in the dark.

Not finding it, Kay retraced her steps. "It's by the stairs. I'll never get used to where things are in this house. Nothing is where it should be. Our house in Tallahassee was so much better." She flipped the switch. The light came on above the long, straight staircase. She placed her foot on the first step. Two dark eyes stared up at her through slits in a ski mask.

Kay screamed, ran to the bathroom, hit the door with both hands, and slammed it shut behind her. She twisted the lock on the handle and fumbled with the phone. Fingers frantically swiping and scrolling her contact list, she touched her dad's number and hit the speaker. Her hands shook, barely maintaining a grip on the phone. "Dad, help, please!"

"What's the matter?"

"There's someone in the house. Come home, please!"

"What? Where are you?"

"I'm locked in the bathroom."

"Stay there. I'm calling 9-1-1."

Pushing with her back against the locked door, Kay sat trembling for more than ten minutes, her heart beating so fast she felt faint. Car doors slammed and voices echoed upstairs. Should she open the door?

"Kay? It's the police. Your parents are here."

Kay cracked open the bathroom door. "I'm up here. Is he gone?"

Her dad shouted, "Yes, it's safe!"

Skipping steps as she descended the stairs, Kay's foot slipped, and she fell to one side.

"Whoa there, young lady," he said.

Kay bolted from her dad's arms and ran to her mother. "I was so scared."

Her dad put his arms around them both. "It's all right. Everything's fine. What happened?"

"I forgot to lock the back door. I started down the stairs and there was someone in a ski mask standing at the bottom."

The police peppered her with questions.

Thirty minutes later, the tall officer asking most of the questions closed his notebook and spoke to Kay. "You probably saw him before he took anything. I think he was here only a few minutes."

The officer turned to Dad. "Based on the time line of when you left and when your daughter saw the intruder, he had limited time to look around. If you find later that he did take something, please call me. Here's my card."

The other younger officer chimed in, "You should keep your doors locked, even when you're home. There are transient burglars roaming from town to town, trying to hit easy targets. The good thing is that the same burglars more than likely won't try this house again."

Kay's dad smiled and nodded at Kay. "I'm sure they won't."

The officers and the family walked into the kitchen. Kay stood between her parents, holding their hands.

"There *is* one thing that troubles me." The tall officer tapped his notebook with the pen. "Since the intruder came in soon after you left, it may be that your house was being watched."

Kay began to tremble.

Her mom drew her close. "It's over. Everything's OK."

Kay fought back tears. OK? Everything's *not* OK.

CHAPTER SIXTEEN

The spoon quivered in Kay's hand. She took a bite of the near soup gelato that her dad forgot in the car when the police were at the house. "I need to call Anna."

Her mom reached out and touched Kay on the arm. "Maybe you should wait and call her in the morning. It's late. She's probably in bed."

"She'll be worried. We were talking before...before..." Kay dropped her spoon in the bowl, and put her arms in a tight self-embrace.

Her mom slid the bowl across the table. "I'll put the gelato in the freezer."

"But, Anna's expecting me to call her back."

"While you get ready for bed, why don't I give her a call and explain what's happened? I'll tell her you'll call in the morning. How's that?"

Kay's mom walked with her to the bedroom and stayed while her daughter put on pajamas. "Try to sleep. I know you're upset. We are, too. This was a frightening experience." Her mom tucked her into bed and punched the light switch.

Kay said, "Would you leave the door open, please."

Her mother cracked the door and walked away.

Kay lay in bed, staring at the reflection of her alarm clock on the ceiling. Five minutes later, the phone rang. Kay hopped out of bed, carefully picked up the phone, and covered the receiver with her hand.

"Hi, Anna."

"Mrs. Telfair, when Kay was talking to me, she cut me off and hung up."

"She's in bed. She forgot to call you back."

"Is she sick?"

"No. She's fine. I think she's very tired."

"Will you please tell her to call me tomorrow?"

"Of course I will."

Kay waited for her mom to end the call, placed the phone on the cradle, and crawled back in bed. "I don't know what I'm doing here. I miss my friends. I only have one friend here. I don't know if she really likes me. And now this thing with the letter." She rolled over, her tears soaking into the soft down of her pillow.

CHAPTER SEVENTEEN

Kay bolted upright. Last night. The man in the ski mask. The police officer asking questions. Her mouth was cotton dry. She reached out but couldn't feel her cell phone. Pulling hard on the charging cord, the empty plug snapped back in her hand. She rubbed her eyes, looked at her alarm clock, and placed it back on the nightstand.

Hopping off the bed, Kay spotted her capris lying in a pile on the floor. The phone. She had put it there when she hung up on Anna and went to lock the back door. More memories rushed forward. Fumbling for the light switch. Staring down the stairs at the man in the mask. Hiding in the bathroom. The police car's flashing lights. She lay back on the bed, taking quick, shallow breaths.

After dressing, Kay put the phone in her pocket and went downstairs. The bold, earthy aroma of freshly brewed coffee hit her nose.

Kay's mom raised her head and laid the tablet computer aside. "Good morning, dear. How did you sleep?"

"Not too bad, but I'm very tired."

"How about some coffee? It's fresh—only a few minutes old."

"Thanks, I could use some." Kay added half and half and a packet of sweetener.

The two sat at the table. No one spoke for several minutes while caressing their mugs and sipping.

Kay's mom refilled her cup. "Your dad's having an alarm system installed next week."

"That won't help if I forget to lock the back door. This whole thing was my fault. I didn't lock the door when I took out the garbage."

"It's not your fault. If someone wants to break in, they'll do it. He could have easily broken the glass or tried some other way to get in. That's why we'll get an alarm."

Kay held the mug, her hands trembling. Coffee dribbled over the rim. "I know, but I made it easy for him."

Her mom hopped her chair closer and put her arm across Kay's shoulder. With the other hand, she wiped the spilled coffee with a paper towel.

Kay's vibrating phone interrupted the quiet.

"It's a message from Anna. I'm going to go to my room if that's OK."

"Sure, go ahead."

Kay sat in the middle of her bed and scrolled down to Anna's number. Before making the call, she took a deep breath. She knew what Anna was going to say, and Anna was right. Kay didn't know what to do. Tears welled in her eyes. She stopped crying, touched Anna's number, and lay back on the pillows.

"What's going on? Your mom said you were tired? We were talking, and you hung up, and you—"

"Wait, wait. Let me explain. When I told you I was going downstairs to lock the door, there was someone in the house. He was standing at the foot of the stairs and was wearing a ski mask."

Kay waited for Anna's response. Nothing. "Anna? Are you there? Anna? What's wrong?"

"What's wrong! You ask what's wrong? Did you tell your parents about our thing—you know, that we took the letter and we had a break-in at my house?"

"No, I didn't. And we don't know if it was the same person who broke into my house and yours."

"Do you really believe that?"

Kay closed her eyes and took a deep breath. "I don't know what to believe."

"Don't you think it's strange that we had a burglary and then you have one? And don't forget, the tube is gone, but we know they didn't get the letter."

Kay pushed her hair back with her right hand and held onto the back of her neck. "How's this? We mail the letter to your dad at the park like we agreed?"

"I think we need to tell our parents what's been going on. I'm scared about this whole thing."

"You're right. Though we won't be allowed out of the house for the rest of our lives after we tell them."

"Do we tell them at dinner tonight? Or after dinner? Or what?"

Kay tapped her chin. "We should tell them together, or else they'll be calling each other and yelling at both of us. We want to get our stories straight. I don't mean that we would lie. We might tell things in a different way or leave something out. I mean—I don't know what I mean. I'm very confused." Kay swung her legs off the edge of the bed and snapped her fingers. "That's it. We'll have a cookout."

"What? A cookout? What's that going to do?"

"At a cookout with our families, we can tell them everything while they're all together."

"And how do we get them to a cookout?"

"You get your mom and dad to invite us over to your house. Tell your mom that it would be a nice gesture to have us over since we're new to New Jersey and that you like me and we have a good time together."

Silence.

"Anna? I said—"

"Yeah, right. We're having a *great* time." The phone clicked.

Kay checked her e-mail and read the message from Historical Research: "I am interested in the document. The details you sent were very intriguing. I would be willing to pay $500 for the letter. Please let me know if you wish to sell."

Kay flopped back in the chair. "Five hundred dollars?"

CHAPTER EIGHTEEN

"It's going to be a hot one." Kay's dad wheeled the car into the Gardino's drive.

Hot? Kay glanced out the window. Anna would be especially hot when she heard Kay's new plan.

Anna's mom greeted them. "How's everyone on this hazy and humid day?" She gave special attention to Kay with a long hug.

Kay returned the embrace as Anna came out of the house. "Excuse me, Mrs. Gardino. I need to speak to Anna." Kay met her friend at the back door, spun her around, and pushed her. "Let's go inside."

"What're you doing?"

Kay poked her in the back to keep her moving. "Shhh. Let's go to your room."

The two reached the bedroom, and Kay closed the door. "He wants to buy the letter!"

"Who wants to buy it? What are you talking about?"

"Somebody from one of the websites I sent an e-mail to. He offered me $500."

Anna's eyes bulged. She gritted her teeth. "I don't care about the money! We're going to give it to my dad and tell our parents what's been going on. That's our plan."

Kay said nothing.

Anna put her face close to Kay's. "Well, isn't it?"

Kay gazed up and half smiled.

Anna, eyebrows raised, leaned in. "Kay, are you listening to me?"

Kay shrugged, lips together.

Anna shook her head. "No, no, no, no, no! You *promised*."

"If we sell it to this guy, it's out of our hands, and we don't get in trouble."

"Listen to me." Anna took Kay's hand and pulled her closer. "You said these burglaries are random. If that's true, why would some burglar only take the tube that held the letter? Why not some valuable stuff, like a TV or a computer?"

Chewing on her bottom lip, Kay tapped her index finger next to her mouth. "I know I said that, but the guy who broke into our house didn't look like the one who made me run off the road."

"Kay, you're confusing me. You said he wore a ski mask."

"Anna, let me see if I can sell this letter. If I can, we won't have to say anything to anybody." .

Anna rolled her eyes and fell back on the bed. "You're not listening to me."

"Let's go outside." Kay grabbed Anna's hand. "They'll think we're up to something."

Anna waggled her head. "Guess what. We *are* up to something."

Anna's mom scanned the yard. "Anna, where's Buddy?"

"He's coming. I told him to turn off his video game and not be rude. He's on his way."

Anna took a seat at the long table. Kay sat next to her. Anna scowled and slid over. Kay bumped shoulders with Anna and whispered, "Stop it."

Anna glided even farther away and sneered at Kay.

Kay caught her dad's gaze.

He gave her his "be-nice" look and turned to Anna's dad. "How goes the burglary investigation at the park?"

"It's slow, very slow. Not much happening, unfortunately."

"No leads?"

"Not a one as far as I know. The FBI is investigating and—" He reached for the iced tea pitcher, poured the liquid into his plastic cup, and paused. "And I'm not sure what's going on."

Kay's dad held out his cup for more tea. "Did the police find out anything about the burglary here? We know nothing about the break-in at our house."

"The police haven't contacted us, but interesting you should ask." Anna's dad squinted at his phone, holding his hand above the screen. "I got an e-mail this morning. It's a police report from one of the crime watch websites. One of our rangers sent it to me. The report says that the township police caught two men riding around the area. The police questioned them and the men couldn't say why they were riding through the neighborhoods. Anyway, they found stolen goods in the car and arrested the men. They were from Delaware. The men said they just picked houses at random to break into."

Kay nodded at Anna and gave her a nothing-to-worry-about look. Anna shook her head and glared at Kay. Buddy sighed, got up, and kicked the soccer ball.

Kay ran over to Buddy, side stepped, and dragged the ball between her feet. "Anna, come on."

Buddy followed Kay. Anna joined them as Kay kicked the ball well into the back of the yard. She jogged over to Anna. "See, we worried for nothing."

"What about that guy running you off the road on your bike?"

"Maybe I was too far into the lane. Maybe he wasn't paying attention."

"Then what about the tube being taken?"

"He thought it was valuable or maybe...I don't know."

Anna shook her head, put her hands on her hips, and pointed at Kay. "You are *not* living in the real world."

Kay put her hands on Anna's shoulders. "This will all be over soon, and, trust me, we won't be grounded."

"I'm not worried about being grounded. I'm worried about much worse."

CHAPTER NINETEEN

"That was a very nice afternoon," Kay's mom said, unlocking the door to the kitchen. "Don't you think so, Kay?"

"Yeah, it was fun." Kay smiled as she jogged through the kitchen past her mom, and ran up the stairs to her room. She opened the laptop. "Where's that e-mail from Historical Research?" She scrolled. Another e-mail popped up from History Collectors, the other site she had contacted: "Thank you for the information about the document. We believe the document to be very valuable and would like to meet and examine it further. We are prepared to offer you $2,000 if the document proves to be authentic. If you agree, please provide a time and a location to meet. Since we have clients around the United States and the world, we can easily come to your location."

Kay sat back and didn't move for almost a minute. She leaned forward and typed: "Yes, I would like to meet. I will e-mail you with a time and place." She hit send, reached for her phone, and called Anna. "Guess what."

"Is this another one of your schemes."

Her mom yelled, "Kay, would you come down here, please!"

"I'm on the phone!"

"Now, Kay!"

"I need to go, Anna. Call you later."

Kay hung up and ran downstairs. "I'm here. What's up?"

"Your dad and I need to talk to you. Let's sit in the family room."

Kay plopped on the sofa. What did she do now? Did she push her parents too far?

Her dad sat beside her and touched her arm. "You seem distant and preoccupied. Is everything all right?"

Things actually were better—except for the letter she took from the ferry house, the bike accident, the burglaries and the…Kay shook her head. "I'm fine, really. I miss my friends in Florida, but, really, I'm OK."

Her mom's tone softened. "By the way, have you heard from any of them?"

Kay frowned and examined her fingernails. "No, I haven't."

"Did you e-mail any of the girls on the swim team?"

"Yes."

"And did they answer you?"

"No. I take that back. One did."

"What did she say?"

"She wanted to know when I was coming back to Tallahassee."

"I see." Her mom frowned at her father.

A tear rolled down Kay's face. "I'll get used to living here. I promise."

Her mom sighed. "And what about Anna?"

"We're good." Kay brushed away the tears. She wasn't sure if Anna was her friend or not. "We get along."

Her mom smiled. "I hope so. You spend an awful lot of time at her house."

Kay swallowed hard. "I…well…you see she has to babysit her brother a lot and it's just easier if I go over there."

"I'm not prying, dear. Just curious. I was hoping you two would become friends."

"I think we're friends. I mean, I want to be her friend." Kay remembered that she promised Anna that she wouldn't get her in trouble over the letter. If there were trouble, that might end any hope of a friendship.

Kay's dad reached for the TV remote. His wife gave him the evil eye. He put down the device. "I detected some friction between you two at the cookout."

Kay sat up straight on the edge of the sofa. There was no way she could explain all that was going on with the letter. "Anna was mad at me today for something. I don't even remember what it was. I'm sure she'll get over it."

Her dad leaned forward, elbows on his knees, and rested his chin on his fingertips. "It was as if you had BO the way she kept moving away from you when you sat down at the table."

"You know us teenage girls. Doesn't take much for us to be crabby."

Her mother left the side chair and sat next to her, pulling her close. "We're worried about you. I know this move has been tough. It's been difficult for all of us. Please tell us when you're feeling sad or if you have a problem. We're your parents. It's our job to be here for you."

"I know." Kay hugged her. "I'll be better." She stood and put her arms around her father. "I'm sorry, Dad."

"Not a problem, dear. Don't be sorry. Be happy, and that will make *us* happy." He fumbled with the remote. "I recorded a Hitchcock film last night. Do you want to watch it with us?"

Kay decided she should humor her dad. She might need some mercy if everything didn't work out with the letter. "Sure. Let's watch it."

Her mom jumped up. "I'll make some popcorn and get some sodas."

Kay grinned. "Is there a teenage girl character in the movie? Maybe someone like me? It would make it more interesting, don't you think?"

Her father adjusted his recliner. "If there were such a character like you, I'm sure she'd be part of the mystery—or maybe right in the middle of it."

Kay's grin faded. In the middle of it? More than her dad knew.

CHAPTER TWENTY

"**W**hy didn't you call me back last night? I sent you a text. I was worried you had some new goofy idea."

Kay punched the speaker icon and laid her phone on the desk. "Anna, I didn't call because we had a family discussion. It was a little intense. After, Dad wanted to watch one of his favorite movies. He thought I would like it and he—"

"Kay, stop. I couldn't sleep last night. What's going on?"

Kay winced as if she were about to feel the needle for her annual flu shot. Knowing how Anna would react, Kay fired off her words. "I got another offer for the letter—two thousand dollars. I think we should go for it."

"Kay, when is this going to end?"

"Soon, if you'll go with me to meet this person. He says they can meet us where we want. Are you with me?"

Silence.

"Anna?"

"I'm thinking."

"I'm going to tell him to meet us at the store near the bridge tomorrow at three. Can you come with me?"

"I'll do this. But if this doesn't work out, I'm telling my dad everything. I don't care what he does to me. I'm a nervous wreck, and I can't take much more of this."

"Agreed. If we don't get rid of the letter, we'll tell our parents the whole story. I'll call you and let you know if he can meet."

Kay punched the end-call icon and found the e-mail from History Collectors. She clicked the reply button, swallowed hard, and let her hands hover above the keys. Her fingers trembled.

CHAPTER TWENTY-ONE

Kay returned to the laundry room after round trip number four to her bedroom.

"What's going on?" Her mom stood by the washer. "I told you I would help you with your laundry."

"No, I want to do this. I want to help you more with the clothes washing and other stuff since you're going back to work."

"I'm not going yet. I need my New Jersey nursing license first. It'll be a few more weeks."

"I know, but I can help you now."

"I appreciate that, dear."

Kay started up the stairs. "I was downloading some photos from Anna, and I wanted to see if they were done." It was a lie, but Kay couldn't tell her mom she was about to sell the letter for two thousand dollars.

On the fifth trip, Kay saw the e-mail, read the message, and called Anna.

"Plans have changed. Can you go the day after tomorrow?"

Anna's voice was weak. "Yes, I'll still go with you."

Kay took a deep breath and slumped in the chair. Her head fell forward, face resting on her fingertips. She was lying to her mother. Was she also pushing her friend too far? Her new friend in New Jersey—her only friend—was more important than the letter. "Anna, you don't have to go with me. I can do this myself."

"How many times do I have to say yes? I'll come to your house after I eat lunch. That is, if I can eat."

Kay flipped her hair behind her ears. "Can you please do one more thing. Could you put the letter in a container that won't leak. I don't want it to get wet in case it rains."

"Yes, yes. I'll find something for your precious letter. Good-bye." The line clicked off.

Kay confirmed the plans with History Collectors, and sent the e-mail: "Day after is OK. See you at 3 p.m. I'll be wearing a blue tank top." Pushing back from the desk, she stared at the computer screen. Within a minute, a reply came back: "Thanks. See you at 3."

"That's it? What does he look like? What will *he* be wearing?"

Kay typed: "How will I know you?"

This time, there was a longer delay. Kay tapped her fingers on the desk, marking the beat to some song she had in her head.

The reply popped up. "I'll find you. Don't worry."

"Don't worry? I wasn't worried before, but now I am. I don't know what this guy looks like. What was I thinking?"

CHAPTER TWENTY-TWO

"**H**ello, Anna, I didn't know you were coming over." Kay's mom unlocked the screen door and let the teen into the kitchen. "I see you have your backpack. Are you and Kay going for a ride?"

Kay stood next to the fridge. "We're going for a short ride. Not long." Kay wasn't fibbing this time. She was just not telling why they were taking a bike ride.

Anna swung the backpack off her shoulder and held it in front of her as she followed Kay through the kitchen.

Kay whispered as they topped the stairs. "Did you bring the letter?"

Anna patted the backpack and smirked. "Of course. Why would I—"

"Sorry. I'm nervous and anxious. Thanks for doing this."

Anna sat on the edge of Kay's bed. "I'm just as nervous. When are we going? I want to get this over with."

"It's only two-thirty. We'll leave in fifteen minutes."

Anna sat wringing her hands. She reached into the backpack for her phone and scrolled through photos. She angled the screen at Kay. "Here's a shot I took at the shore last weekend."

Kay dropped her bike helmet on the bed and sat next to Anna. She needed to calm her friend. "Is that Buddy buried in the sand? I can't tell."

"That's him. My dad does that to him every summer at least once. Here's me with Mike, the lifeguard. I met him last summer. He's seventeen." Anna swiped through a dozen more photos.

Kay put her arm on Anna's shoulder. "Great photos. I hope we get to the beach—I mean, shore—this summer. And I want to see more of your photos, but we probably need to get going."

Anna tucked her phone in her capris, shook her head, and took a deep breath. "I can't believe we're doing this."

Tiptoeing through the kitchen, Kay held Anna's hand while Anna carried the backpack with the plastic container and the letter. She pushed open the back door and ran to her bike. "Hurry. We don't want to miss the guy if he shows up ahead of time."

The girls pedaled for about ten minutes, stopping at the intersection across from the convenience store.

"Tell me again who we're supposed to meet."

"I don't know. He'll find us. He wouldn't tell me how I'd know him."

"So, we wait for some stranger to walk up to us—or to you?" Anna shook her head, her eyes wide. "This is crazy."

"I told him I'd be wearing a blue tank top."

"You're doing that for sure. It's almost glowing. Not exactly a fashion statement."

"I wanted to make sure I was noticed."

"You'll be noticed—trust me."

Kay huffed. "Anna, please. You're annoying."

Anna rolled her bike back a few feet and away from Kay.

Kay eased off the seat and stood beside the bike. "I'm a little nervous."

"*You* are? My hands are shaking."

The light changed. The girls walked the bikes across River Road and up to the parking area near the store. Kay took the container from Anna's backpack and sat on the curb under a large oak tree.

Anna paced in tight circles. "What time is it?"

Kay picked up her phone. "Two minutes till three."

"Do you think he'll show?"

"He said he would."

Anna reached in her pocket and held three crumpled one-dollar bills in her hand. "I'm going inside to get a soda. Want something?"

"No, thanks."

Kay watched Anna walk to the store entrance.

A man stopped near the door and looked past Anna and back at Kay. Nearly colliding with Anna, the man waved at a passenger in a black sedan parked on the side of the store. Walking to the car, he glanced back over his shoulder several times.

Kay cradled the container, checked the time on her phone, and watched for Anna to come out of the store.

Anna pushed open the door, holding a soda. A woman walked by with the man who had almost bumped into her earlier. Anna stopped the door from closing and held it for the couple. The man and woman brushed by her and hurried down the sidewalk toward Kay.

Kay stood. Could one of these people be the person who would buy the letter?

CHAPTER TWENTY-THREE

"We're from the FBI, the Federal Bureau of Investigation."
Kay's mouth fell open. She stared at the ID, then at the woman, who was taller than Kay and wore black pants, a black jacket and a white shirt.

The woman asked, "And your name is?"

Kay swallowed the last few drops of saliva in her mouth. "Kay. My name's Kay."

The man showed his ID. "We're confused. Are you here to sell an old letter?"

"I…well…my friend and I, we came to meet somebody who said he wanted to buy it. Am I in trouble?"

The woman looked back at Anna. "Is that your friend?"

Kay motioned to Anna.

Anna pointed her finger to her chest and mouthed, "Me?"

Kay answered with exaggerated nods of her head.

Anna hesitated. Slowly, she ambled toward Kay, who stood between the man and woman.

Kay grabbed Anna's hand and drew her close. "This is my friend Anna. We came here together."

"Hi, Anna. I'm pleased to meet you. I'm Terri."

Anna trembled, her mouth wide open and her eyes glazed over.

"This is Marty. He's a data-forensics specialist," Terri said.

Kay asked, "He's what?"

"He's an expert with computers." Terri showed her ID to Anna. "As I told your friend, we're from the FBI."

Anna staggered backward. "I need to sit down. I don't feel so good."

Marty held the girl's hand as she sat down on the curb.

Kay swallowed hard. Her gaze darted back and forth between the woman and man. "I know what the FBI is. You're the government police." She reached down for Anna's soda, took a sip, and handed it back to her, coughing. "Am I under arrest?" Kay pointed down at Anna. "She didn't do anything. It's all my fault."

Terri slid her ID into her jacket pocket. "Yes, we are like the police, and, no, you're not under arrest. We're here to help you."

Kay handed Terri the container.

The agent opened it and gave the letter to Marty.

He unrolled it and held up the document. "Did you steal this from the park visitor center?"

Kay's eyes widened. Her mouth dropped open once again. She glanced at Anna and then stared at Marty. "What? No, we…I mean, *I* took it from the ferry house. We saw a man working on the fireplace, and he found this letter in a container."

Marty put the letter back in the box. "This container?"

Kay gestured with her hands to show the size and shape. "No, it was in a metal tube. It was really heavy."

Scratching his bald head, Marty shrugged.

A dark-gray, four-door sedan stopped in the front of the store. A man stepped out, arms high, palms up, and shoulders arched. "What's happening here?"

"I'm not quite sure," Terri said. "This, or rather, these are the people we were to meet. Girls, this is Agent Stanton. He's from the FBI office in Trenton." She turned to Kay and Anna. "Girls, I didn't get your last names."

"I'm Kay Telfair, and this is Anna Gardino."

Terri glanced down at Anna. "Is your father the superintendent at The Park at Washington Crossing?"

Anna jumped up. "Are you going to tell him? Am I in trouble?"

"I'm not sure. That may be up to your father." Turning to Agent Stanton, Terri said, "I don't think we need you today. Thanks for your help. Marty and I will take care of this. I think there's been a misunderstanding. I'll fill you in tomorrow."

Terri waved as the agent drove away and then focused her attention back to the girls. "I think we should go to the park and speak to Anna's dad."

Anna shook her head and frowned at Kay. "You promised no trouble."

Kay bit her lip and clasped her hands in front of her. "I'm sorry, Anna, I didn't think that—"

"Why do we need to talk to my dad?" Anna asked. "Can't we give you the letter, and we'll go home?"

"I could do that, but I think I need to know more about this letter you found. I suggest we put your bikes in our car, and we'll all go over to your father's office at the park."

Anna pointed at the FBI car. "We aren't supposed to get in a car with strangers, and we're supposed to tell our parents if someone offers us a ride."

"You're right. You should call your dad and tell him that some FBI people are bringing you over to his office. Kay, do you want to call your parents and let them know?"

Kay's eyes bugged. "If Anna calls her dad, that will be enough?"

Terri nodded. "That makes sense. Let's talk to Anna's dad first and see what we need to do."

Anna took out her phone. "Hi, Dad. The reason I'm calling is that some FBI people want to give Kay and me a ride to the park. No... wait...let me explain...I'm fine. Kay's fine."

Terri whispered to Anna, "Let me talk to him."

"Mr. Gardino, Agent Terri Keenan here...No, they're fine. Yes, of course. I'm not sure what this is all about. I can explain better in person why I'm here...No, I don't believe there's any reason to be alarmed. Do I have your permission to transport Anna and Kay to your office? Thanks, we'll be there shortly. Yes, I will. Good-bye."

Kay opened the door of the car and slid across the backseat.

Anna eased in and closed the door. Tears welled in the corners of her eyes. "Kay you promised me."

Kay let her head fall forward, leaning on her hands. "I'm sorry, Anna. I'm really sorry."

CHAPTER TWENTY-FOUR

The ranger at the reception desk ratcheted his gaze from face to face, coming back to Anna. "Hello, Anna. Did you have a good ride through the park? I see you have your friend with you again." He focused on Kay. "Sorry, missy, I don't remember your name."

Anna scowled and blurted. "Her name is Kay, and and she used to be my friend."

Kay whispered, "I said I'm sorry. I didn't know we'd be arrested by the FBI."

Terri leaned toward Kay. "You're not being arrested. Everything's going to be fine." She flashed her ID at the ranger. "We have an appointment."

The ranger's eyes popped.

Anna yanked open the staff-only door. "I'll take them back. It's this way. My dad's office is down the hall."

The group stood at the open doorway of the superintendent's office.

His back to the door, Anna's dad held the phone to his ear. "They said the girls were not in any trouble. Wait, they're here. I'll call you in a few minutes." He swiveled his chair around and hung up the phone. "That was my wife, Anna's mother."

Terri displayed her ID. "I'm Terri Keenan. We spoke on the phone. This is my associate, Marty Smith. We're from DC."

"I'm Rich Gardino. I'm the superintendent here—Anna's dad." His mouth drawn tight, he stood and walked around the group. "Let's go to the conference room next door."

On the way to the conference room, Anna eased up next to her dad and put her arm around him.

He hugged her and patted Kay on the shoulder. "What's this all about? Did my daughter do something wrong? Are the girls in trouble?"

Terri laid her briefcase on the table. "Let me explain what I know. The reason we're here is because we've been working on the case of the stolen artifacts from your visitor center."

Anna's dad sat between the two girls. "I was told the FBI considered me a suspect, but I don't understand why. And I don't know what the girls have to do with it."

Marty put his arms on the table and leaned in. "A few weeks ago, we set up a dummy website and got e-mails from this area from someone who wanted to know the value of a historical artifact." He took the letter from the plastic box and held it up.

Terri said, "We couldn't get the exact address, but it was near the park." She nodded at Marty. "I put that in one of my reports, and my supervisor told us we should include you as a possible suspect."

Throwing his hands in the air, the superintendent's face glowed red. "I had nothing to do with the burglary. And I hope you don't think my daughter took the items. That's impossible! I know the FBI believes it may be an inside job, which is ridiculous!"

As the color in his face returned to its normal outdoor, tanned look, Terri smiled at him. "I'm sure we'll get to the truth about the girls' involvement. There's an explanation, or, more correctly, multiple explanations. As Marty said, we set up this website to buy historical artifacts. We received an e-mail with some interesting content."

Anna's father glanced at his daughter, who cleared her throat and glared at Kay.

Kay squirmed. The birds chirping outside the window gave her an excuse to turn away. Anna punched her with her index finger.

Terri removed the letter from the container. "We began an e-mail correspondence with someone who said he or she had a letter and wanted to know its value. Since we didn't have any leads or suspects in the center break-in, the FBI decided to pursue this lead. The person who e-mailed us sent a rough transcription of this letter." She showed it to Anna's dad.

He unrolled it and read. "This doesn't look like anything that was stolen. I've gone over that list many times. I'm 99 percent certain."

Terri nodded. "I came to that conclusion, too. By the way, there's some considerable interest by one of your US senators who's been pushing us to solve this case."

Rich leaned forward, elbows on the table and fingertips rubbing a small mole on the side of his chin. "Yes, I'm quite aware of the senator's interest."

Terri motioned to Anna and Kay. "Let's have the girls tell us what they know. Who wants to begin?"

Rolling her head back to catch a deep breath, Kay's mouth tightened. "It's all my fault."

"Go ahead," the agent said. "Tell us what's been going on."

Frowning, Anna's dad said, "I don't mind you asking Anna questions, but don't you think we should have Kay's parents here?"

"You're absolutely correct. Kay, let's call your parents?"

Rich stood. "I have an idea. Let's go to my house, and from there I'll call and invite them over. We can all hear the explanations at the same time. I have a feeling this is going to be very, very complicated."

CHAPTER TWENTY-FIVE

"**W**hat's going on?" Buddy squinted and stared at the two agents.

His mom patted him on the shoulder. "Buddy, these people are from the FBI in Washington. They're like the police."

He glowered at his sister and Kay. "Is this about the letter?"

Kay rolled her eyes. Anna closed hers and shook her head.

"It was Kay. She took it. But she was just trying to make my knee feel better."

Mrs. Gardino's mouth fell open, and her face went blank. She shifted her gaze from Buddy, to Anna, and, finally, to Kay.

Terri put her hand on Buddy's shoulder. "Do you know something about the letter?"

"I know some stuff."

Kay avoided eye contact with Buddy and fidgeted with her cell phone.

"With your permission, Mrs. Gardino, I'd like Buddy to stay. He may have some information that could be helpful."

Buddy's mom pointed him toward the sofa. "Would you sit by Anna, please?"

Kay's mom and dad arrived. Her mom rushed over to her. "Are you all right? What happened?"

"I…I…I was the one who took the letter."

Kay's dad shifted his focus from the FBI agent to Kay. "What letter?"

"Mr. and Mrs. Telfair, we're talking about this letter." Terri opened the container. "This is my associate, Marty Smith, and I'm Agent Terri Keenan. First of all, your daughter's not in trouble—at least not with the FBI."

Terri explained why she and Marty were there and how they had met the girls. "And it turns out the letter is not one of the stolen items. That's all we know at this point."

Buddy's eyes grew big. He jumped off the sofa. "Are we in trouble?"

Terri chuckled. "I don't think you're in trouble with the FBI, but you may have to explain some things to your parents."

"Kay and Anna were just trying to help me when I—"

"Let me tell you what happened." Kay stood. The details came in a flood of words. "It all started when we were in the park and Buddy fell off his bike. I said we should go in the ferry house and get some water to put on his skinned knee. I knew we weren't supposed to go in there because of the construction."

Anna's dad glared at his daughter. Shoulders drooping, Anna sunk back into the sofa.

"Mrs. Gardino, may I have some water, please?" Holding the glass in both hands, Kay took a sip. "We were upstairs watching the man fix the fireplace. He didn't know we were there. We saw him pull a metal tube from a hole in the bricks. The man opened the tube and took out a piece of paper and read it." Kay took another drink and gazed at Anna. "He was excited and said something, but I didn't understand. Before he left, he put the paper back in the tube and hid it. We went downstairs, and, on my way out, I took the tube and brought it home."

Kay's dad scowled at her.

Her Mom shook her head. "Why didn't you turn this in to the park?"

"If I did, Anna would be grounded because we were told not to go into the areas where the men were working."

Rich rolled his eyes, winced, and caught his wife's frown.

Terri focused on Kay. "Then after you found the letter, you went online to sell it?"

Anna jumped in. "I wanted to mail it to the park. Kay wanted to wait until we saw how much it was worth."

"I was curious." Kay shrugged. "And if it was valuable and we turned it in, you wouldn't be mad at us."

Anna's voice rose. "Then the man who found the letter in the fireplace tried to run over Kay!"

Kay's dad yelled, "What!"

"I think he only wanted to see who I was, Dad. I lost control and ran off the road on my bike. The letter inside the tube was in my bike bottle holder."

Terri stood. "Kay, how do you know it was the man at the ferry house?"

"I saw the hat he wore when we were in the house. It was blue and yellow and looked like a duck's head. When I saw the hat, it startled me, and I crashed. Some lady was jogging, and she helped me."

Kay's mom asked, "You weren't racing around the yard on your bikes when you scraped your knees?"

"No, ma'am." Kay sat down next to Anna and swallowed. "I wasn't racing."

Anna took a deep breath and blurted out, "Then our house was broken into, and the tube was gone from underneath my bed."

Anna's dad jumped up, his face glowing red. "The money on the counter wasn't the only thing taken in the break-in?"

Anna grabbed Kay's hand. "Yes, and Kay saw the man driving up her street one day when she put out the trash cans."

"I'm confused," Terri said. "Let's back up. There's a lot going on here." She took a deep breath. "Someone broke into your home?"

Her dad glared at Anna and shook his head. "Yes, but only a few dollars were taken—or so we thought. The police said it probably was a random burglary. You know, the economy's bad, and burglaries are up."

Kay's mom glanced at her dad and then focused on Terri. "Our home was broken into a few days after."

"Too many coincidences here." Terri tapped her finger on her chin and pointed at Kay. "So you decided to sell the letter when we offered you two thousand dollars. Correct?"

Kay leaned forward and sat on the edge of the sofa. "At first some-one offered us five hundred dollars."

"You had another offer? What did you tell them about the letter?"

"The same thing I told you."

"And where was this person who wanted to buy the letter?"

"In Princeton. I found the place on the Internet. There was only a post-office box."

The parents said nothing.

Terri panned the room, looking at each of them. "It seems the only things the girls are guilty of are breaking some of your rules and maybe fibbing to cover it up. Girls, would you mind going to Anna's room? I want to talk to your parents. Buddy, would you go with them, please?"

The trio headed for the stairs. Halfway up, Kay raised her hand and pressed her finger to her lips.

Terri said, "Thank you all very much for being patient and understanding—both with Marty and me and with the kids. I know this has been a nerve-wracking experience. What Kay and Anna have told us has been very helpful. But I need to ask Kay's parents for some more help. Would you allow me to use Kay's e-mail address to contact the other website that wanted to buy the letter?"

Kay's mom said, "I don't understand. Do you think there's a con-nection with what the girls did and the park break-in?"

"I'm not sure," Terri said. "There may be some connection with the park worker and the other website that offered to buy the letter."

Kay's dad looked puzzled. "What makes you think that?"

"It's only a hunch and a long shot at best. Using Kay's e-mail to correspond with the other website, we may discover more leads on the park burglary."

"That's acceptable, as long as she's not involved and her name isn't used." Kay's dad nodded at his wife. "When do you want to do this?"

"Right away. This evening, if possible."

"Why do you need to do this tonight?" Kay's dad asked.

Terri glanced at Marty. "We're getting a lot of pressure to solve this case. Also, you may not be aware, but Mr. Gardino was a suspect and I know he's anxious to get this mess cleared up."

Kay and Anna stared wide-eyed at each other.

Buddy bolted down the stairs.

"Buddy," Anna whispered, trying to grab her brother by the arm.

Too late. He raced into the room. "Are we going to help find out who broke into the visitor center?"

His mom held him gently by the arm. "Were you listening?"

Kay and Anna joined the group.

Anna jerked Buddy by the arm and gritted her teeth at him.

Mrs. Gardino put her arm around Anna and stroked her hair. "I have an idea. It's dinnertime. I have some meatballs in the freezer, and I can cook some pasta. Anyone interested?"

Buddy rubbed his stomach. "I'm really hungry."

With nodding all around, the moms went to the kitchen.

The two dad's sat on the sofa, chatting.

Terri, Marty, and the girls gathered in Rich's home office.

Marty set up his computer. "Kay, show me the e-mails from the other site that you contacted about the letter."

Kay logged on and scrolled through several e-mails, stopping on the one with the five-hundred-dollar offer.

The computer specialist read the e-mail and sent a reply: "Do you still want to buy the letter?"

Terri peered over his shoulder. "Let's see if we get a response. We don't know if he'll reply tonight, but you never know."

Kay backed away from the computer. "What if he says he's still interested?"

"I have a plan," Terri said. "Let's test him."

Kay stared at the screen. "Do you think the person who wanted to buy the letter stole that stuff from the visitor center?"

"I don't know, but it's unlikely."

"Do you think maybe he bought the stuff that was stolen?"

"A possibility."

Anna put her hands to her cheeks. "When you catch him, will you—"

"Let's take this one step at a time." Terri leaned in toward Marty's computer. "I have a hunch that things are going to get pretty interesting before this is over."

CHAPTER TWENTY-SIX

Talk over dinner brought more questions from Kay. "Is that what FBI agents do, follow leads?"

"Among many other things," Terri said.

"How long have you been an agent?"

"Five years."

Buddy jumped in. "Have you shot anybody?"

His mom almost choked. "Buddy! That's not appropriate for the dinner table."

Buddy caught his mom's glare and winced. "I think I'd like to be an FBI agent. Wouldn't you want to be an agent, Anna? How about you, Kay?"

Anna stared into the office.

Kay laid her fork in the plate and leaned back. "I wouldn't mind being an agent. It sounds exciting." She saw the raised eyebrows around the table. "What? I said I wouldn't mind. I didn't say I was going to enlist or whatever you do to join."

Terri chuckled. "You have a long time to think about your career, Kay. One skill you certainly would bring to the FBI, and that's interrogating people."

"Sorry about all the questions."

"Not a problem. When I was in high school and interested in engineering as a career, someone gave me a quote from Albert Einstein. I remembered it all through college, and it's served me well at the FBI. Einstein said, 'The important thing is not to stop questioning.

Curiosity has its own reason for existing.'" Terri pointed at Kay. "So keep asking questions."

Marty excused himself and stepped into the office. He yelled back, "Jackpot. We got a response."

Terri and the girls joined him.

He read the e-mail aloud: "Yes, my offer still stands."

Terri pointed her index finger in the air. "Let's see if we can get more information from this guy." She leaned in closer to the screen, nudging Marty away from the keyboard, and typed: "I am located in Central New Jersey. Where are you?"

A few minutes later, the response came back: "That's convenient for me. Can we meet?"

Terri sent a reply: "Yes, we can meet. I have been researching the document's value, and I would like $10,000."

Thirty seconds later, the response: "What would you do with $10,000? That's a lot of money. I can pay you more than my original offer, but $10,000 is not possible."

Marty eased around Terri to view the screen. "What does he mean, 'What would you do with $10,000?' That's an odd question, don't you think?"

Kay waited for the agent to say something. Marty stared at the screen.

Terri sat back in the chair. "Let's think about this. Why would he say that? I think he's angry that the price is being upped, and he knows who he's dealing with—a teenage girl."

Kay's eyes widened. Her jaw dropped. He knew she had the letter. He knew who she was.

CHAPTER TWENTY-SEVEN

"I wanted that one!" Buddy pointed at the pastry on Anna's plate. Sitting at the kitchen table with Buddy and Anna, Kay whipped her head around. "Shush, you two. I'm trying to listen." She quietly slid her chair closer to the dining-room doorway.

"I still don't understand," Anna's dad said. "What's the relationship to this buyer and the park break-in?"

"I'm getting to that. There was an emotional response in one e-mail. The sender asked why she, the seller—meaning Kay—would want $10,000. The next e-mail stated he would pay more but that $10,000 was too much. I said that this was my final offer and that I wanted the money for college. My sense is that he knows that Kay or Anna has the letter. That's why he initially questioned Kay about wanting that much money. There's only one way he knew one of the girls had the letter: either the worker at the park told him, or it's the worker who's operating the website."

Anna's dad rubbed his head from front to back. "The police questioned every staff member and construction worker. All their alibis checked out."

"Sometimes alibis are faked, and we in law enforcement aren't perfect. But, like I said, I still want to follow this lead to see where it takes us. I'm expecting a response tomorrow if not later tonight."

Buddy tapped a spoon on the table. "Are you and Kay going to be grounded?"

Anna closed her eyes and shook her curly head.

"I think we're done with this whole thing," Kay said. "The FBI has the letter. Our parents know all about what we did. We have to wait and see what happens."

Anna plopped her elbows on the table and put her face in her hands. "I don't know what my parents will do to me. I was already on shaky ground."

Kay touched her friend on the arm. "Whatever the punishment is, we'll survive."

Anna took a long sip of water and put her elbows back on the table. "Sure, we'll survive, but I'll be grounded for the rest of my life."

Buddy patted his sister on the arm. "If you get grounded, I can run errands for you."

"That's very kind of you to do that, Buddy. *Isn't it, Anna?*"

"Sure. Fine. Whatever."

Kay grabbed Anna's shoulders and leaned down to look her in the face. "Don't worry. Everything's going to be fine."

Kay's dad yelled from the dining room, "Kay! Anna! Would you come in here, please?"

Kay sighed and rolled her eyes. "Or not so fine."

Her dad said, "Girls, Mr. Gardino told me he needed some extra help at the visitor center."

"That's right. I have a storage room where we keep literature and some display materials. It could use some reorganizing. Plus, the displays in the visitor center need dusting and straightening. I had to cut back on the cleaning service—budget cuts, you know."

Kay's dad winked at Rich. "In light of your latest escapades, girls, we hoped you would be willing to help out. Say, for the next two weeks."

Anna gave Kay a look that would melt steel.

Kay glanced up at the ceiling and angled her head toward Anna. Raising her shoulders and opening her palms, Kay gave a weak smile.

Anna made a low, growling sound and stomped out of the room.

CHAPTER TWENTY-EIGHT

"**I** hate getting up this early." Anna slammed the door of her dad's truck.

Kay winced. "I'm sorry. I didn't think this would happen."

"I agree. You didn't think."

"Are you going to be mad at me the whole time we're working here?"

"I don't know. I'll have to think about it."

Rich held the door at the employee entrance. "Let's go, ladies. You have a lot to do today, and I have to get ready for the FBI folks. They'll be here soon."

Anna's dad laid his briefcase on the desk. The ranger at the reception desk stuck his scraggly gray head in the superintendent's office.

"Eddie, Kay and Anna are going to help us for the next two weeks. Would you show them to the storage room? It's a mess, and they can start there."

"Sure, but I need to—"

"And work them hard. They're free labor." Anna's dad chuckled.

"Dad!" Anna's eyes bugged. "That's not nice."

The ranger stepped inside and pointed out into the corridor behind him. "I've been trying to tell you, Millie's here."

"What? Millie? What's she doing here? I have an appointment in five minutes. Did she say what she wanted? Tell her I'm busy."

Eddie stepped back from the doorway. "Oops, too late."

Rich lifted his gaze from the stack of papers on the desk. "Good morning, Millie. I'm surprised to see you here. I didn't see you on my appointment calendar."

Kay and Anna stood outside the storage-room entrance across from the superintendent's office and the conference room.

Kay shifted around Anna for a better view into the office. "Who's that?"

"Millie Richards. She's president or something in the Preservation Society. My dad says she's not very nice."

Millie brushed Eddie aside. "Where're the FBI agents? Why didn't you tell me they were coming?"

"I didn't know until late yesterday," Rich said.

"I received a call last night from the senator. He's been getting updates on the investigation."

"I didn't want to bother you until we knew more. Of course I'll call you."

Eddie stood in the office doorway. "The other board members are in the conference room."

Anna's dad's mouth dropped. He stared at Eddie and glowered.

Millie stepped between the two men. "Eddie, please bring some coffee and tea to the room."

The girls eased inside the storage-room door as Millie walked out of the office.

Thirty seconds later, Anna's dad stormed out of his office and slammed the door behind him. With her head sticking out into the corridor, Kay felt the breeze as he walked by and burst into the conference room.

"Good morning. You're here early," Terri said."

Kay spun around. "What? I didn't see you come down the hall."

"I said, 'You're here early.'"

Anna stepped into the doorway. "Yep. Too early."

Terri smiled. "I'll talk to you both later. I need to speak with Anna's dad."

Terri entered the conference room.

Kay shuffled across the hall and stood at the door.

Anna called out in a low voice, "What *are* you doing?"

Kay waved her over. "Come on. Let's listen."

Terri placed her briefcase on the table and tapped the superintendent on the shoulder. "What's happening?"

He drew close and told her about Mille Richards. "The board is expecting a report from you. Evidently the senator got a message from the FBI that you were here investigating the burglary."

Millie walked up. "Are you the FBI agent?"

Terri whipped around and introduced herself.

"May I have your attention, please?" Millie tapped the table with the end of her pen. "This is Terri Keenan from the FBI in DC. She wants to tell us about the progress of the investigation."

"Good morning. Superintendent Gardino requested that we come to New Jersey to help with the investigation of the park burglary."

"*Dad* invited them?" Anna whispered to Kay. "Really?"

"I think she's saying that to be nice to your dad so it doesn't look bad. You know, the burglary and people saying he was involved."

"Our investigation is still ongoing. However, we have very few leads. You may recall, there were no fingerprints found and no other evidence from the scene that would help us. That's about all I can tell you."

Millie stood and took a deep breath.

Anna glanced at Kay. "Here it comes. Millie's a real crab. She hates dad."

Kay recoiled at the sound of footsteps shuffling up behind her and turned around. A man put his finger to his lips and smiled. "Shhh. I want to listen, too."

Millie nodded. "Thank you, Agent Keenan. I would have expected more progress from the FBI and the park management by this time. But I suppose we'll have to continue to wait for the burglary to be solved—and to have repairs made to the center." She glared at Anna's dad. "Does anyone have any questions?"

An older woman with purplish-gray hair spoke up. "Why do you think this investigation is so difficult?"

Terri stood. "The burglar was either very sophisticated or very lucky. No usable clues were found at the scene. But we'll follow all leads, no matter how small."

The woman continued, "With such a small amount of information or leads, why send the FBI?"

Terri glanced at the superintendent and winked. "Millie's husband, your senior US senator from New Jersey, has taken an interest in this investigation. Senator Richards cares very deeply about his state, and that holds true for this very important historical site. He wanted us to make sure the FBI was doing all it can to bring this investigation to a satisfying conclusion. Wouldn't you agree, Millie?"

"Why, yes…yes, certainly." Millie's frown broke into a halfhearted smile. "Absolutely, I agree."

"Of course, maintaining the FBI focus on this incident is due in large part to Millie's initiative." Terri picked up her briefcase and stepped away from the table. "Rest assured we'll keep Chairwoman Richards and the board informed of our progress."

Kay and Anna inched inside the conference room and stood by the door.

Millie scowled at two of the board members who got up and walked to the coffee service. Others began to chat. "Well…I…I suppose that's all we needed to hear. Thank you for coming."

Terri spotted the girls and walked in their direction. One of the members stopped her. "I wanted to ask if the FBI has traced any of the stolen items."

"We have not. Do you have an interest in such artifacts?"

"Not professionally. I'm an attorney. Name's Ed Bigelow." The man shook Terri's hand and gave her a business card. "I believe strongly in preserving our history. I also serve on the board of the Princeton Historical Society."

Terri read the card, winked at Kay, and returned to the conversation. "What do *you* think happened to the stolen items?"

"I have no idea. That's why I asked you."

Terri said, "They could have been sold to someone who wants them for their private collection. There's a growing worldwide market for historical American documents."

"I wasn't aware of that. I didn't realize anyone outside of the United States would have an interest." The man checked to see who was nearby.

Terri hesitated, and waved at Kay and Anna. "Excuse me. I need to speak to someone."

Kay watched Bigelow walk toward the coffee service. He turned and stared at Kay. She inched closer to Terri. "Why was he interested in the stuff that was stolen?"

Terri pinched her lower lip between her fingers. "I'm not sure. Maybe he was genuinely interested or..."

"Or what?" Kay asked.

"I don't know. It's probably nothing." Terri shook her head and glanced back at the man. "Maybe my FBI training makes me naturally suspicious."

CHAPTER TWENTY-NINE

"You're late. The meeting's over." Millie scowled at Colin Vandekirk, who walked around Kay standing at the main door.

Anna's dad and Terri left the conference room through the second door. Anna stepped out of the storage room and called out, "Are you coming back in here to help me?"

"Shhh. I can't hear what they're saying."

Anna joined her and craned her head over Kay's shoulder.

Kay motioned toward the table with the coffee service. "Let's go over there and pretend to clean up. We can listen better."

The girls slowly stacked the cups, and moved the napkins and sweetener to different areas of the table.

Colin shook his head. "My apologies for being late, Millie. I was outside the door and heard most of the presentation. And, frankly, I'm somewhat disturbed about how this investigation's being handled. We didn't hear anything new. Maybe this was a waste of time. I mean a waste of time for the FBI to come up here."

Ed Bigelow drank a few sips from his cup and shuffled closer to Millie and Colin.

Millie shrugged. "Perhaps."

"I agree." Bigelow took a step toward Colin and Millie.

Millie frowned at the man.

"I think this investigation is at a dead end," Colin said. "And it may prove to be embarrassing for your husband."

"How's that?"

Colin touched Millie's arm. "If it gets out that the senator urged the FBI to go after this case, it may look bad. This is not a situation of national importance."

Millie pursed her lips. "I didn't consider that. He *is* up for reelection next year."

"It's something to think about. You've done a marvelous job of leading the Preservation Society. But it may appear that the senator is asking the FBI to use resources at the request of his wife."

Millie put her hand to the side of her face. "You're right. That's excellent perspective. Plus, this agent didn't offer much hope. Thanks, Colin."

"You're quite welcome. You know how much I'm committed to the society and certainly want the senator to be around for another six years at least." Colin raised his eyebrows. "Maybe there's a management problem here at the park."

Anna jerked her head back. "What!"

Kay elbowed her in the side. "Listen and be quiet. And don't stare."

"But—"

"Anna, please. Let's just listen."

Bigelow moved closer to Colin. "I think these artifacts are gone for good. If the superintendent had been doing his job, the break-in wouldn't have happened."

Millie tugged on Colin's arm, pulling him closer. "I must talk with the senator about this immediately. I'm not confident in Superintendent Gardino's ability to handle this. He did hire Eddie—that incompetent ranger. We think he didn't set the alarm in the visitor center the night of the burglary. That's why whoever broke in did it so easily."

Bigelow jumped in once more. "Perhaps you should have the senator get the FBI to back off the investigation."

Colin nodded. "That's an idea, and maybe the senator could help us get a new superintendent."

Millie folded her arms. "Perhaps it's time for some changes."

Anna gritted her teeth. "Why that—"

"Shush," Kay whispered.

Bigelow leaned in toward Millie. "Do you think the senator could use his influence to replace the superintendent? Doing that might offset any bad publicity about him pushing the FBI investigation."

Colin jumped in. "Plus you'd get credit for straightening out this mess and getting the park in the hands of proper management."

"You're both very astute," Millie said. "And very valuable members of our board."

Kay and Anna watched as Millie and Colin walked out. Bigelow looked around the room and ambled over to the table with the coffee service. Kay lowered her head. Anna stared as the man approached. Kay pulled her by the arm. Bigelow tossed his paper cup into the trash, bumping the table with his leg. Startled, Kay turned around. Bigelow stared, waiting for Kay to speak.

She brushed past the man. "Excuse me. Come on, Anna. Let's get back to the storage room. Your dad will be mad if we don't finish straightening the place up."

Bigelow stepped between the girls. "So, your dad's the superintendent?"

Kay grabbed Anna's arm and turned her away from the man, not letting her answer.

Outside the conference room, Anna brushed off Kay's grip and ran straight to her dad's office with Kay close on her heels.

Terri entered the office behind the girls and shook her hands loosely in front of her. "How was my presentation? By the way, you're out of paper towels in the ladies' room."

"What? I'll get Eddie to—"

"Dad!" Anna whipped around the desk.

"Not now."

"But, Dad—"

"Anna, please. I'm trying to talk to Agent Keenan. Have you finished in the storage room and restocked the pamphlets at the reception desk?"

"We're working on it, Mr. Gardino." Kay gently nudged Anna out of the office.

Anna whispered, her shoulders drooping, "I have to tell him."

"Later. I don't think this is a good time. In fact, I wouldn't tell him ever."

Standing at the reception desk, Kay and Anna sorted pamphlets.

"Those comments from Millie about my dad really bother me."

"I know they do, but your dad doesn't need to hear this stuff now."

"You're probably right."

Kay put on a devilish smile. "Of course, I'm right. Aren't I always?"

"Yeah, sure. You're always doing the right thing. That's why we were almost on the FBI's most-wanted list."

CHAPTER THIRTY

"**I** love this—a nice office job." Kay chuckled. "I can't think of anything else I'd rather be doing during my summer vacation."

Anna picked up a stack of brochures. "If this is what an office job is like, I don't want one." She handed the brochures to Kay. "Here, Ms. Telfair, put these in the plastic holders."

Terri and Rich entered the visitor-center lobby and stood at the display cases to survey the damage done by the burglar.

Marty burst into the reception area, balancing a laptop on his left arm. "We got a reply. The buyer will go up to five thousand dollars."

Kay stopped straightening a stack of brochures and leaned on the counter.

"You have to see this." Marty took a deep breath. "We need to act tonight."

Anna's dad stuck his head close to the laptop screen. "What do you mean by 'act tonight?'"

"Wait." Terri surveyed the room. A few visitors lingered at the displays. Terri put her finger to her lips and whispered, "Let's go back to your office."

Anna stared at Kay, eyes wide. "Yeah, what do they mean 'act tonight?'"

"I don't know," Kay said. "Let's find out."

Anna slowly opened the door to her dad's office. "Mind if we listen?"

Rich moved from the computer screen. "If the FBI approves."

Terri nodded and again read the e-mail, this time aloud for the girls. "I'm willing to pay five thousand dollars. That's my final offer, but I must have the document tonight."

"The time stamp was only a few minutes ago," Marty said.

Anna folded her arms. "Why does he want to do it tonight?"

Terri slid the laptop in front of her. "Maybe he's got a buyer on the hook." She hit reply: "5,000 sounds good. I don't know if I can make it tonight." She sent the e-mail and sat back. "Let's see what happens."

Several minutes passed, then the reply came: "It's either tonight, or the deal is off."

Terri went to the keyboard again: "Sorry. That won't work for me."

Two minutes passed. Terri bit her lip.

A reply popped up: "I'm sorry, too."

"Looks like we pushed him to the limit. Let's try this. Terri laid her fingers on the keyboard: "I looked at my schedule again. I can make it at 8 p.m. Let's meet at the store next to the Washington Crossing Bridge. Do you know where that is?"

Terri read the reply: "I will find it with my GPS. How will I recognize you?"

Kay looked over Terri's shoulder as the agent typed: "I will be wearing an orange shirt."

"*You'll* be wearing an orange shirt?" Kay's eyes widened. "*You're* going to meet this person?"

"I'm about your height—maybe an inch taller. I can get away with being a teenager. It'll be getting dark by then."

Marty made a few keystrokes and popped his head up from the keyboard. "Dark by 8:17, to be precise."

Anna's dad leaned on his desk. "And what are you going to do when you meet this guy?"

"I'll be wired so I can talk to Marty and Agent Stanton. I'm going to let the buyer see the letter and take his money. After that, I'll surprise him by flashing my badge."

Kay grinned. "I remember when you showed us your badge. Yep, this guy's in for a big surprise."

CHAPTER THIRTY-ONE

"**A**nna. Call me." Kay ended the voice mail and sent a text message. She noted the time on her phone: 7:09. "Where *is* that girl?" Sitting on the edge of her bed, she tapped her fingers on the back of her phone and flipped it over twice to check the time.

Anna's ringtone sounded.

"Finally!" Kay said. "Where've you been?"

"Just out to dinner with my parents. I think my dad felt guilty about making me work at the visitor center today."

"Great. That's terrific. I had leftovers. I guess my parents weren't feeling that guilty. Listen, I'm going to go down to the store at the bridge and watch the FBI meet this guy."

No response.

"I said I'm—"

"I heard you! Now please tell me why you want to do this."

"I'm curious. I told you I might want to be an FBI agent someday. I think Terri's awesome."

"Kay, I've only known you for, what, about a month. I know that's not a long time to get to know someone, but you are something else."

"What do you mean?"

"I can't figure you out."

"Hmmm. That's what Mom says."

"There. That's my point. You drive everybody crazy with your wild schemes. Someday it's going to spell big trouble for you."

"More than being stopped by the FBI?"

"Yes, much more than the FBI thing, as bad as it was."

"I understand how you feel, but will you go with me?"

"Do I sound like I want to go? I'm your friend and I want to stay your friend, but I can't do this. It's crazy."

"It's not crazy. All I'm going to do is go down to the store and sit across the street and watch."

"I'm sorry, Kay. I won't do this. Don't you think you've pushed your luck far enough?"

Kay sighed. "If you won't go, will you do something for me?"

"What?"

"I'm telling my parents I'm going to your house for a few hours. Can you cover for me?"

"Wouldn't they call you on your cell phone first?"

"Probably. But in case the call doesn't go through for some reason, my mom will definitely call your mom."

"It's going to be dark by the time you get home. What do I tell them if they do call and are worried about you?"

"Just say I'm on my way. I should be home by dark. Terri said the meeting with the buyer won't take long."

"This confirms it, Kay. You're insane."

"Will you cover for me?"

"Yes, yes. I'll do it, but promise me you won't do anything stupid. You know, it's just as hard for me to make new friends." Anna chuckled. "It was hard enough for me to get to know you. I've invested a lot of time here."

Kay smiled. "I understand. Don't worry. You know me."

That's what worries me, Kay. I *do* know you!"

CHAPTER THIRTY-TWO

A truck rumbled down River Road, stirring up a light cloud of dust. Kay straddled her bike at the intersection. She squinted, covered her face, and watched the light change. Walking her bike to the row of trees across from the convenience store, Kay sat by the bike trail in the lush, dark-green grass and waited. She checked the time: 7:33.

Five minutes later, a voice from behind startled her. "Hello."

Kay jumped up, her heart pounding.

A man and a woman slowly pedaled by her on a tandem bike. The woman breathed heavily. "I could use a rest myself."

Kay smiled, waved, and returned to her vigil.

The rays of the low evening sun found openings in the trees and hit Kay in the face. She blocked the light with her hand, moving her head until she found the shadows. The dampness from the river rolled over her in the still evening air. She stared at her phone: 8:06. The whirring and whining of tires on the metal roadway distracted Kay from her watch. Three cars came off the bridge, one right after the other. The cars' tires thumped as they cleared the metal roadway and bounced on the pavement. The sound reminded Kay of the dull thud of balloons banging against each other.

Kay watched the store. Agent Stanton's dark-gray sedan slowly turned into the parking lot by the store. Wearing an orange blouse and jeans, Terri got out of the passenger's side, and the car sped off down River Road.

The lights in the parking area in front of the store came on. Kay had a clear view from the shadows of the trees.

Five minutes passed, then ten, and then fifteen. Terri held tight to the container with the letter. She looked left and right and repeated the motion at least five times.

A rust-eaten, brown van stopped in front of the store and a few feet from Terri. Kay gulped. The FBI agent took a step off the curb.

The van's engine sputtered.

Terri handed the container through the passenger-side window. The vehicle accelerated. The agent stepped back, nearly tripping over the curb.

The van wheeled out of the parking lot in the direction of the bridge.

Terri lowered her head, lips moving.

Kay's eyes widened.

The brown van smoked and bucked, coming to a stop thirty feet from the bridge. The driver tried several times to restart the engine. Two cars pulled up behind him. He jumped from the van, holding the container. Looking back over each shoulder, he ran onto the bridge walkway.

Kay yelled, "Somebody stop him! He's getting away!" She hopped on her bike and pumped the pedals. Approaching the bridge, she slammed the brakes. Her back tire streaked a ribbon of black rubber across the sidewalk. Her heart raced. Riding bikes on the walkway was illegal, but that was not her biggest problem. The bridge—the metal monster—scared her. She swallowed hard, took a deep breath, and eased onto the narrow pedestrian path. The handlebar and pedals barely cleared the sides. "Where's the FBI?" Gritting her teeth, she stood on the pedals, closing the distance between her and the man. Kay struggled to keep the bike in the middle of the narrow path.

The man passed in and out of the lights and shadows. His boots clomped on the walkway planks. He threw a glance over his left shoulder.

The reflection of the FBI car's flashing lights bounced off the girders ahead. Kay chanced a look back. Her bike wobbled. The left pedal clipped the lower rail of the walkway. The bike cartwheeled her over the top. She grabbed the rail and hung on by both hands. Seventy feet of humid air separated Kay from the murky water below. She closed her eyes, hands and fingers burning from the tight grip. Swinging her legs side to side, she fought to find a foothold that wasn't there. "Help me! Please, somebody!"

The phone vibrated in her capris. She looked down at her pocket. It was probably her mom calling to find out where she was. If only she were at home and not hanging off that bridge. Kay blinked to clear her vision. "Please help me, I…I'm…" Kay stared into the darkness below. Her left hand ached. Her grip loosened.

"Hang on!" a male voice yelled.

Snapping her head up, she stared into the face of the man she had chased onto the bridge. Her eyes grew wide. Her mouth fell open.

The man's hands gripped her wrists. "I've got you."

With a joint-wrenching tug, he pulled her up and over the rail, set her down on the walkway, and knelt beside her.

Agent Stanton grabbed the man's arm. "Stand up, and put your hands behind your back. You're under arrest!"

Terri ran to Kay's side. "Are you all right?"

Kay panted and rubbed her right hand. "My wrist hurts a little."

Terri poked the man in the chest with her finger. "Please take care of this joker, Stanton. I'll take care of the young lady."

Terri supported Kay's arm and helped her stand. "What in the world are you doing here?"

"I came to watch you do your FBI sting."

"Watching is one thing, but why did you chase the guy?"

"I saw he was the man who ran me off the road. He was getting away. I didn't see you or anybody going after him. What happened when he drove up?"

She turned to the other FBI agent. "I'll walk Kay back off the bridge. Take this guy and the plastic container back to the van. We'll meet you there."

"Wait," Kay said. "My phone rang while I was…I was…." She looked back at her bike lying on the walkway and pulled out her phone. "My mom called. I'd better call her." Kay tapped on the phone. "Hi, Mom. Yes, I'm on my way home now. I'm with Terri and Marty. I wanted to see them catch the man who was going to buy the letter. Yes, ma'am. I know I said. . .yes. . .Here's Terri."

Kay winced and handed the phone to Terri.

Terri nodded, and smiled at Kay. "Mrs. Telfair, she's fine. Yes, she came down to watch. No, I didn't know. Yes, we caught the guy. Of course, I'll bring her home shortly. You're welcome. Good-bye."

Kay and Terri ambled down the narrow wooden path. Kay stumbled, steadied herself, and held onto the rail and the agent's hand.

"You asked about what happened at the store. When I stepped toward the van, the driver told me to hand him the document and then he would give me the money. I moved closer and shoved the container through the passenger window. Before I could flash my ID, he took off. I tried to call Agent Stanton, but he couldn't hear me at first. Something must have blocked the radio signal."

"Did you get the money?"

"No. The driver probably never planned to pay for the letter." Terri held Kay's hand as the two stepped off the end of the walkway. "Do you want us to take you home now?"

"I'm fine. I want to stay and find out if this is the guy who broke into my house and Anna's house."

Terri squeezed Kay's hand and walked her to the van. "Stanton, let's search this rust bucket."

Stanton punched the switch on a small flashlight and climbed in the van. Terri and Kay moved closer to the open back doors. He panned the light around the inside and rummaged through tools and trash. "This thing is heavy." He waddled in a slight stoop to the door and handed a plastic bag to Terri.

Terri took the tube out of the bag.

Kay rubbed her fingers along the rough surface. "This is the tube the letter was in."

Terri held the tube in front of the man, who stood handcuffed to the van's side mirror. "What's your name?"

The man stared at the lead container.

"I said, what's your name?"

"You have my driver's license. Don't you know it already?"

Terri tapped the tube and put her face a few inches from the man's. The man arched his head back. "Trevor…Trevor McNally."

"Why didn't you give me the money when I handed you the letter?" Trevor smirked.

"I asked you a question, Trevor."

Still no response.

"I think I know. You thought you could keep the cash that some-one gave you to buy the letter. And you figured some little teenage girl couldn't do anything about it. Right?"

The man shuffled his feet and coughed. "Whatever you say."

Terri held up the tube. "Where'd you get this?"

"I found it."

"Where did you find it?"

"Somewhere."

Kay tugged on Terri's arm and whispered, "Ask him about the ban-dage on his arm. They think the burglar at the park cut himself on the broken glass. There was blood on the carpet."

Terri pointed to the bandage. "What happened there?"

"Cut my arm."

"How?"

"Working."

"How about when you broke into the park's visitor center?"

"I'm not saying anything."

Agent Stanton leaned in and whispered.

Terri nodded and put on her serious FBI face: furrowed brow, lips tight, and squinting. "The young lady here says you tried to hurt her and caused her to fall over the rail."

Kay touched Terri's arm. "But—"

Terri shook her head at Kay. The agent stuck her right index fin-ger in Trevor's face. "You might be facing some serious charges here."

Trevor's eyes bugged. "I didn't do anything to her. I saved her!"

"That's not what we saw. But if you answer our questions, maybe we can clear up this misunderstanding."

"No jail?"

"I didn't say that. Maybe not *as much* jail time."

"I took the container from somebody's house." Trevor smacked his lips. "I need some water. There's a bottle on my front seat."

Terri held the bottle to his mouth. "Did you break into the park's visitor center?"

"I'm not answering that."

Again, putting her face close to Trevor's, Terri pointed at Kay, shaking her head.

"Listen, this was not my idea. I know a guy who buys these things. He told me he would pay me some big bucks for stuff from the visitor center."

"What things?"

"You know, these old letters and things."

"And he bought the things you stole from the park?"

Trevor let his head slump. "Yes."

"Who is this guy?"

"I don't know his name. We meet somewhere, or I call him, or he calls me."

"What does he look like, this person you sold the artifacts to?"

Trevor described the man.

Terri and Kay stared at each other. Kay's eyes grew big. She shook her hands in front of her. "Are you thinking what I'm thinking?"

Terri nodded. "Yep, and I know how we can wrap up this investigation in a hurry and ease the stress on Anna's dad." She took the cell phone from her jeans and punched in Mr. Gardino's home number. Waiting for him to answer, Terri gave Kay a thumbs-up.

Kay took a huge breath and exhaled slowly.

"Mr. Gardino, Terri Keenan here. We need to talk."

CHAPTER THIRTY-THREE

"I can't believe they let you come in here after last night." Anna held the outside employee-entrance door for Kay on their second day of work at the park visitor center.

"Mom and Dad wanted me to stay home. Terri told them what happened. But they were so glad I didn't get hurt that they sort of forgot about the rest. I told them I was feeling all right. Besides, Terri said she wanted me and you here this morning. There's a meeting of the Preservation Society."

Anna squinted at Kay. "Why us?"

"Not sure?" Kay knew why, but she didn't want to alarm Anna. She had put her friend through enough tension in the past few weeks.

The girls caught up with Anna's dad, who was standing at the entrance to the conference room. Tools, large pieces of glass, and boxes lined one wall, with the table and chairs shoved to one side.

Kay pushed by Anna and walked in. "What's going on?"

The park superintendent surveyed the room. "That's what I'd like to know." He leaned back into the corridor. "Eddie!"

Eddie scurried down the hall. "What's wrong?"

"We're having a society meeting here this morning."

"Two days in a row? I didn't know about any meeting."

"I set it up last night. Why's this stuff here?"

"The men are here to fix the displays. Millie can now stop her complaining."

Rich shook his head at the mess in the room. "Bring the chairs from the conference room to the lobby and set them up. Have the men knock off work. The members will be here in an hour."

Anna touched her dad's arm. "We can help. What do you want us to do?"

"Help arrange the chairs in the lobby." He spoke to the ranger. "And please set up a coffee service there, too."

● ● ●

Anna's dad pointed at two chairs in the front row. "Anna, you and Kay sit over there."

Anna moved toward the end of the row of chairs. "Do we have to speak or do anything?"

"No speaking. Only listening. Agent Keenan and I thought you might find the meeting interesting."

The two girls sat. Anna whispered to Kay, "Interesting? Really? This is the society board meeting. Dad hates these things. Do you know what this is all about?"

"It's a meeting of the Preservation Society. That's all I know."

Kay took a quick glance over her shoulder. Her heart pounded. She sat on her hands to stop them from shaking. Ed Bigelow and Colin Vandekirk had taken seats directly behind the girls.

Terri arrived and went straight to Millie, who stood in front of Kay and Anna. Terri winked at the girls. "Good morning, Millie."

Millie broke off her conversation with Anna's dad. "Good morning, Agent Keenan. I spoke with the senator yesterday, and he hopes this investigation is coming to a conclusion."

Terri gave a weak smile. "It looks as though it has come to that, Millie."

Rich reached for his cell phone. "Excuse me, I need to make a call." He stepped away, returning after less than thirty seconds. "We're ready to begin."

Millie positioned herself in front of Terri and turned to face the group. "I see that everyone's here. My apologies for calling meetings so close together. Thank you all for coming, once again, on short notice. However, I think we have some good news. As I told each of you in my phone call last night, the investigation into the visitor-center burglary is being terminated. For more on this, we'll hear from—" Millie stared at Rich, who waved at Millie and pointed at Terri.

"Thank you, Millie. As you said, the investigation is coming to a close. But it's not because we have no leads. It's just the opposite. In fact, we've made one arrest."

Millie's eyes opened wide. She took in a quick breath and let out a quiet gasp. She sat speechless, looking up at Terri. A low murmur from the other members filled the room.

"It's only been a little more than twenty-four hours since we arrived here to follow up on the break-in. In that short time, we uncovered some information that will help us close this case. First, though, I want to recognize two special people who helped us with this investigation: Kay Telfair and Anna Gardino. Kay recently moved to the area with her parents from Florida, and Anna is the daughter of the park superintendent. Thanks to them, we were able to get the critical information we needed to solve this crime."

Terri paused, focused on the entrance doors, and nodded. Agent Stanton and Trevor walked in. Chairs squeaked as everyone turned to see who had entered the lobby.

Anna tapped Kay's shoulder. "Who's that?"

Kay didn't want to turn around. She'd have to look at one of the men sitting behind her.

Anna whispered, "You're not looking. Is this the guy the FBI caught last night?"

Kay hesitated. She glanced back and then returned her gaze forward. "Yes. That's him." Kay also saw the expression on one of the men—surprise and panic. She swallowed, her mouth dry and heart racing once again.

Stanton stayed at the back of the room, his hand on Trevor's arm. Kay watched Terri, who stared intensely at Trevor.

Trevor gave Terri a quick nod. Stanton led the man outside, returned, and stood in the back of the room.

Terri said, "These two young women recovered a significant historical artifact found here in the park."

A woman in the back row asked, "Is it one of the stolen items?"

"No. Anna and Kay discovered the item in the Johnson Ferry House. It was hidden in a secret compartment in the fireplace that was being restored. I sent a copy to a friend who is an expert on the Revolutionary War. I wanted him to authenticate it and analyze its contents." Terri removed the rolled-up letter from the container and held it up. "This letter was written only a few days before Washington crossed the Delaware in December 1776."

Ed Bigelow stared at his watch. "What does this have to do with the things that were stolen?"

"I'm getting to that. But I'm sure the society members would like to hear a little about this piece found right here in your park."

Millie smiled and nodded.

Terri unrolled the document. "The letter was supposed to be delivered to the commander of the Hessian troops in Trenton. Unfortunately, we don't know who wrote it. The signature is not readable. The letter offered a Christmas truce to be made between Washington's army and the Hessians to ensure that no attacks would be made over the holiday. We don't know why the letter was hidden and not delivered. My expert gave several explanations of why this letter was composed. One being that it may have been a trick to lull the Hessians into complacency. None of this matters. We all know what happened."

Terri paused and looked at Anna and Kay. "The girls found the letter while exploring the ferry house, and searched the Internet for background on the document. A dealer in such artifacts contacted them and offered to buy the letter. The man we arrested last night in our sting operation broke into the center and sold the stolen artifacts to this dealer. The man also broke into the girls' homes to try and steal the letter. But, when that failed, we believe the dealer used the man to buy the letter from the girls. That's when we caught him."

Terri told the society board members about Kay showing up at the FBI sting operation, Kay's attempt to follow the man, and the bike accident.

Kay blushed and squirmed in her chair.

Terri walked over and put her hand on Kay's shoulder. "Fortunately, Kay was not injured, but her bravery certainly helped the FBI bring this case to a close."

"I need some coffee." Bigelow got up and bumped Kay's chair, jostling her and causing her to lurch forward. He leaned down to Colin. "How about a cup? I'm going to get some." Despite his efforts to whisper, his deep voice filled the room.

Millie scowled. "How rude."

Colin coughed lightly and cleared his throat. "Yes, I think I'll have a cup, too."

Kay drew her right shoulder up and took a peek behind her. Colin circled behind a row of chairs and glanced back at the visitor center front door.

Terri waved at Stanton. Kay whirled her head around, following the action. Stanton moved over in front of the door, blocking the entrance.

Colin shuffled quickly toward the table with the coffee and cut off Bigelow. He bypassed the table and headed for the staff entrance. With a rush of air, the sharp edge of the heavy metal door collided with Colin's shoulder and forehead. The impact knocked his glasses off. He backpedaled and collapsed on the floor.

Eddie held a small tray with both hands and peeked around from the other side of the door. He winced and raised his shoulders. "Oops, sorry. I forgot the creamer and napkins, and I was in a hurry."

Terri knelt beside Colin. Blood trickled from the man's brow. Kay, Anna, and the superintendent stood over Terri and Colin.

Eddie handed Terri a wad of napkins. Terri grabbed the stack and pressed it against the man's head. "Colin Vandekirk, you're under arrest for accepting stolen federal property and aiding and abetting in the theft of such property. You have the right to remain silent—"

"I woulda paid you $10,000. But you didn't need the money, didja?" His speech slurred, Colin raised his hand and pointed at Kay. "*Didja?*"

Startled, Kay shuffled back. "What did he say?"

"He's disoriented, but he confessed indirectly that he operated the website." Terri lifted the napkin from the cut on Colin's head and pursed her lips. She looked up at Kay. "I ran a check on his finances. Colin is in debt up to his eyeballs. I guess he was desperate for money and saw the park as an easy target. With Trevor's confession, this case is wrapped up."

Terri finished reading Colin his rights while the other society members stood and gawked.

Kay stared at Colin, her heart pounding.

Anna put her arm around her. "It's over."

Kay slipped her hand into Anna's and squeezed.

Terri yelled, "Did somebody call the paramedics? It's a nasty cut and maybe a concussion." She twisted around and smiled at the girls. "Thanks for helping solve the case, ladies."

Anna's dad stepped up beside them. "I'd better explain to Millie and the others what's going on."

"From the expression on her face, that would probably be a very good move." Terri took the first-aid kit from Eddie, tossed the napkin, and applied a thick bandage to Colin's head.

The superintendent gathered the board members in a tight circle and explained what had happened. Stepping back to the gathering around Colin, he said, "I have a question I need to ask these two young ladies."

Kay swallowed hard and closed her eyes.

Facing the girls, Rich took Anna's left hand and Kay's right, pulling them close. "What have you two learned from all this?"

Anna shook her head at Kay and grinned. "Next time, I'll pick a best friend who's not so crazy."

Anna's dad chuckled. "And what about you, Kay? What have you learned?"

Kay hesitated. She looked around the room and then focused on Anna. "I learned two things. First thing I learned was how hard it is for someone to be my best friend." Kay put her arm across Anna's shoulders. "And I'm lucky to have one now."

Anna blushed. "What's the second thing you learned?"

Kay gazed around the room. Looking at Colin, she touched her forehead, gave a devilish smile, and pointed at the staff entrance. "You *don't* want to stand near that door."

The End

ABOUT THE AUTHOR

Sonny Barber developed an interest in American history at an early age, reading and collecting newspapers, magazines and other materials on historic US and world events. He's coupled that interest with his fiction writing to create a modern-day "mystery history" series for preteens and older. Sonny graduated from Georgia State University with a degree in journalism. His work as a writer, editor and photographer has taken him across the United States and to many other countries. He and his wife live in South Florida. They have two daughters, who provided some of the inspiration for the teenaged characters in his books.

Made in the USA
Charleston, SC
04 February 2015